freckled face:

# *#Fuck Cancer*

# freckled face:
## #Fuck Cancer

**tamika jorai**

13TH & JOAN PUBLISHING

WWW.13THANDJOAN.COM



13th & Joan books may be purchased for educational, business, or sales promotional use. For information, please email the Sales Department at sales@13thandjoan.com.

First Edition Printed, January 2019

Library of Congress Cataloging-in-Publication Data has been applied for.

ISBN: XXXXXXXXXXX

behind every freckle is
the cure for cancer.

# *table* of contents

In the fascinating melting pot that is New Orleans, marvels a neighborhood known as the Garden District. It's where the culture is vibrantly bursting, the historic mansions stand strong, the Mardi is Gras, the gardens are lavish, and the palate is spicy. It's also where you'll find me, the black sheep, tied up to the superbly shaped tree that shades the grounds of the Dubois manner. Although there is no physical rope keeping me bound to the oak, it's where I send myself to escape the crazy voices and add to my "Daddy wasn't there" chronicles. It isn't the people in my head that I seek refuge from; me and them were cool. I'm trying to get far away from the dysfunctional contents of my home—well as far as my Wi-Fi signal will allow. My mother and brother are fucking aliens sent to this planet to push me over the line of insanity. They truly leave me no choice but to act out and shine bright enough to hopefully catch the attention of my absent father. Clearly he was smart enough to get away. Or even better, I'll hit up Angelina Jolie; I'd absolutely volunteer as her next adopted tribute. Until then, or in the event of an equal miracle, I remain the oddball member of the Dubois family.

"Chance, as much as you would love to die of a heatstroke in this Louisiana oven, I don't have the time for your dramatic symbolic gesture. Get up and get in this house, now," my well-to-do mother aggressively spoke from the porch. Her tone may have had something to do with the newest stain I added to her distinguished reputation that day at school—who knew that proclaiming that I was a unicorn in a shitty field of donkeys over the school's intercom would get me in so much trouble? I got up and walked in the direction of my next punishment, agonizingly crossing over the mat that continuously welcomed me home to the fuckery.

# friend or faux

Day one of my 170-day prison sentence was upon me. The annoyance of my parole officer's voice ricocheted off my eardrums and landed on my last damn nerve as she drove me twenty minutes away from my New Orleans neighborhood to the correctional facility. I needed to break free; it was now or never. I was going to open the door, fearlessly jump from the moving car, strategically tumble through traffic, and eventually roll on to freedom. If this were a movie, and I was Jackie fucking Chan, it may have worked. In reality, my elaborate plan of escape involved rolling down the window to relieve the suffocation of self-loathing. The fresh air invigorated my face, but couldn't remove the not-so-transparent words, "fuck my life" sketched across my forehead in permanent marker. Her condemnatory voice ran off the new laws of the land. She was everything but encouraging; less rules and an ounce of support would have been nice. But just maybe she was having a bad day and I should have been more understanding of her position. I'd probably be a bitch too if I'd stuck my tampon in the wrong hole.

"…don't embarrass me, or I'll absolutely humiliate you." I tuned back in at the finale of her patronizing lecture. Oh, did I mention the enforcer of my incarceration was my very own mother—or so I was told? It was beyond my comprehension as to how we were actually related. I mean, sure, there is a picture of her in a hospital bed holding a Cabbage Patch Kid that marginally resembled me, but that proved nothing. My demands for a paternity test were continuously denied.

"Mom, I don't deserve this," I whined as a last-ditch effort to plead my case, while my loving parental ignored my cries to check her makeup and perfect first lady hair in the rearview mirror. But things weren't always as they appeared; the sugary Michelle Obama persona was just a shell that masked her Cruella de Vil core. My mother may not have been on the hunt for soft furry puppies, but she was definitely on a mission to exile a single black sheep…me. She was listed in the social registry as Sophie

Lynn Dubois: well educated, highly respected, elegant, a celebrated positive asset to society, and a royal pain in my ass. I didn't inherit her mirrored image of polished perfection; the extent of our resemblance came down to a similar pinky toe. I was a modest, breezy girl, happy with whichever way the wind blew, effortless in beauty with giant and wild midnight hair that spiraled from the root and reached for the sky. My nonchalant silhouette featured fitted jeans, sneakers, and if the tee underneath my favorite hoodie wasn't wrinkled, it was considered upscale. I was forced to deal with her for life's necessities, like a home and Wi-Fi, and she was obligated to put up with me for the tax write-off. I'd accepted that her repugnant love was inevitable and our relationship, if any, took more energy out of her than me. I bit my tongue, bowed down, and held my breath for the day when a little loving Lasik would correct her tainted view of her only daughter.

"Excuses are for those who wish to be excused, and those who aspire to be excused are inhabitants of inconsistency…now get out." She ruled with an iron hanger, and I pacified Mommie Dearest by rolling my eyes as I exited the car.

My journey from puberty to adulthood was rocky and rebelliously self-inflicted, so there might have been a small chance I deserved this. My crime can be described as intense adolescence with two scoops of harsh sarcasm, a dash of disrespect, oh, and bad grades were the cherry on top of my shit flavored sundae—in other words, I was a typical ungrateful teenager. My punishment was one year on death row, or what my transcript docs listed as private school. Mommy wrote an extremely large check and, voila, I bypassed the admissions process of applications, interviews, and tests. Cash will trump a winning cynical personality and below-par intellectual effort every time.

"Private school is an unnecessary excursion. I should be enrolled in college with peers of equally matured capacities." It was an endless battle trying to prove that I was a thirty-year-old woman locked inside a sixteen-year-old's body.

"You might have an old soul, but you're a young, delusional girl who couldn't pass as a mature adult, let alone pass a damn equivalency test. Now, go before you're late." She spoke to me unfiltered, without kid gloves and then used those same contradictory gloves to stick her controlling hands up my puppet ass. I may have felt wise beyond my years, but my level of reading and math literacy had yet to catch up. But I was focused on developing in other more critical areas of my life. The life skills I'd ingested didn't come from the mundane classroom textbooks; they derived from watching Saved by the Bell and Flashdance, reading Stephen King and Sunday paper comic strips, and listening to Salt-N-Pepa and '90s R&B classics. The informative combination of the eighties and nineties surely preceded me, but shaped me into an old, been there and done that, black woman. Be that as it may, it was time to woman up and take my punishment.

I stood before an ancient structure that was surrounded by a creepy, magical mist—I was immediately convinced that my mother had dropped me off at Hogwarts. I turned to give Sophie an evil look, but she didn't stick around to shower me with love and inspiration on my first day of school. If I ended up losing my virginity to Harry Potter, she'd have to take the blame and help raise our magical baby. My feet trod over the oak planks that filled the twenty-five thousand square foot school. Every step filled the empty halls with noise that had become chilling, yet irritating, music to my ears. It had to be like a hundred years old; there were even fireplaces featured within the handcrafted picture-framed walls. The paintings of someone's ancestors' ancestors dressed the building, and they hauntingly stared at me as I passed. I jumped at the ring of the school bell that dismissed a mass of students from their first period classes—apparently I was more than just late. An excess of five hundred boys and girls journeyed the halls. It was like looking at my depressed reflection; all of us identical in unimaginative standardized uniforms. Although, I believe I was the only one suffering an allergic reaction to the cloned materials, anxiety plagued my body. No one truly looked happy to be there. They must have known something I'd yet to experience (like the two headed dragons in the dungeon or the meatless burgers being served at lunch). Eventually I found my class and settled into the slacker's section: the back row. I immediately longed for the customarily unsupervised, blasé, as-long-as-you-pass-scholastic structure my old public school offered. Obtaining new and uninteresting information quickly became monotonous and dreary. And given that I was two weeks behind my classmates, I was expected to get caught up at warp speed. I mostly just shook my head in lethargic agreement. My teacher was about as engaging as the nearby kid who pulled a booger from his nose and watched it dry before he put it back into his body. Between his late breakfast and the procedural monotone details from the eldest in the class, I almost fell asleep. But just when I thought my allergic reaction and infinite boredom would be the death of me, Olivia delayed my funeral.

"Today we're going to continue with our debate presentations. Ms. Olivia Joseph you chose to argue Senator Johnson's political stance on the negative influence of homosexuality in leadership roles—the stage is yours for your opposing arguments. This should be interesting…keep it clean." My new Political Science teacher, Mrs. Hamilton, seemed uneasy about giving Olivia liberty to speak. Her apprehension moved me to sit up with anticipation. An immense natural afro framed Olivia's head and smooth milk chocolate dressed her skin. While we all wore stiff, white blouses, she rocked a "Beyonce for President" heather grey T-shirt beneath her cardigan. She accented her pleated skirt with Wonder Woman knee-high socks, giving life to our mandatory mundane apparel.

"Greetings, today I'll be challenging the mind-numbing politician Johnson who allowed his narrow views to escape his small brain." She hadn't prepared any notecards; only self-belief and a passion for the topic poured from her glossed lips.

"My name is Carpay Munch," she announced with confidence. The class giggled.

"How charmingly ghetto, Olivia…clean, keep it clean." Our teacher took the remaining contents of her coffee cup to the head—vodka I presumed.

"When I'm elected to an executive branch of government, eating pussy won't encumber my ability to positively influence public policy and decision making." She was a complete, inappropriate, over the top rebellious activist, and my spirit animal.

"Alright, that's enough Ms. Joseph. You can go share your presentation with the dean." Our teacher dismissed her before I could properly introduce myself as her new, easily influenced best friend. She was just the right amount of irresponsible excitement that would keep me from dropping out of school and finding a sugar daddy on Craigslist's personal ads.

I journeyed the halls in search of the dean's office and unintentionally found a dinosaur when I arrived.

"What the hell are you doing here?" Ruby Rutter was a callous bag of bones former teacher of mine who still held a grudge against me from when I attended Harrison Middle School. Her old ass never found it in her heart to forgive me for adding a few, or ten, laxatives to her morning coffee. Her true hate came from the super glue Stacey Dixon generously spread all over her chair that kept her from making it to the bathroom before shitting her stockings. She blamed me entirely for my squad's prank, even though she had no proof of who conspired against her; but holding my nose me every time I passed her probably gave me away. After all those years, our disgust for one another was still mutual.

"Are you here to embarrass me into early retirement?" Mrs. Rutter didn't appreciate our epic reunion. And who was she kidding, early retirement for her would have been around the time Jesus rose from the dead.

"It's so good to smell you again, but I'm not here for you. I'm here to bring Olivia her lunch, since she's being held captive without proper nourishment during her state appointed lunch break. Would you like to be a part of my statement when I contact the school board?" I placed my hand over my nose as she rolled her eyes and walked away about her business.

"No one has ever spoken to the great-grandmother that way, you've got some balls kid," Olivia spoke up from the wooden bench she waited on just outside of the dean's door.

"Raggedy Rutter is your great-grandmother...my bad."

"Naw, not mine, but I'm sure she reproduced back in the 1800s. Why else would she hate kids so much unless she was tortured by her own? So, where's my lunch? I know they're serving meatballs and Tater Tots today." I didn't really intend to bring her lunch; it was just a ruse to get past the dragon lady. I did, in fact, hoard some Tater Tots in my pockets when I left the lunchroom. Unfortunately, only a few greasy crumbs were left behind.

"When I didn't see you in the lunchroom, I started a long journey to find you—I got hungry on the way. Sorry." I unzipped my book bag and offered up my last piece of gum as payment, presenting a dowry in exchange for her friendship.

"I like your style, kid. I find you enchantingly con-niving, and you have a pulse, which is much more than I can say for the immature and dreary skeletons roaming this damn cemetery they call a school. If you're still hungry, you can join me for a real lunch as soon as I talk my way out of this jail." She accepted my gift, unwrapped the piece of strawberry twist Trident gum, and tossed it in her mouth.

"My name is Chance and you just officially unfucked the fucked, thank you." I bowed my head as a sign of respect and held out my hand—to which she didn't shake; instead she reached for my cell phone and began to make a phone call.

"Hello Pizza Hut, I need a delivery to Ben Dover Preparatory School." Olivia ordered our pizza that was soon delivered to a side door of the school. We swore loyalty to each other over the ceremonial mingling of tomato sauce in the back of the girl's locker room, officially making us blood sisters. My mother's plan clearly backfired—here she thought she was throwing me into a pit of uppity wolves, in the hopes that structured education and stature would rub off on me; when in actuality, I was going to rise victorious with my spirit animal by my side. Olivia was a complete freak and undoubtedly separated from me at birth; I had found my cotton candy unicorn. Over time, we became closer than two boobs, Oprah & Gayle, and ultimately, Kanye & Kanye. Our only interpersonal conflict arose when our menstrual cycles synced, but other than the identical hormonal imbalance thing, we were the epitome of best friends. Our friendship went on to do remarkable things throughout that school year. We won the award for reckless comradery with a purpose; it was easier to change the world with an accomplice than to be punished alone. Sometimes world peace came right after harmless teenage warfare and just before detention. We were the hallmark of teenage recklessness.

There was that one time we engaged in a fight for proper nourishment amongst our peers. Olivia convinced me to call a taco truck to the front of our school and chain ourselves to the tires; she insisted it had to go down on a Tuesday or the impact wouldn't have been as severe. Our efforts to stress the importance of tasty and cost-effective food in our school was celebrated by the students, but punishable by the dean of students. Arguing that the customary neglect of our Mexican friends and other cultures that shared common taste buds was a racial slap in the face, fell on deaf ears. We were slapped with a two-day suspension, but lived to fight another Taco Tuesday.

Operation Free Kermit was a preservation mission to liberate the Muppets legend and return him home to Sesame Street. The dissection of a frog's internal anatomy would destroy our childhood educational memories; there was no way I could cut open a frog that taught me how to count. We fought for our rights by sneaking into the biology class early morning of the scheduled dismemberment and dumped the caged amphibians into our backpacks. We stashed them in our lockers and high-fived each other when the teacher was forced to play a video in lieu of the dissection lab. Regrettably, we met some friends at the mall after school, leaving our bags to overheat in the car for four hours. Our forget-table rescue and prolonged exposure to the high temperatures proved deadly. I guess frog lives didn't really matter after all.

Our last notable offense hampered any chance of a proper birthday celebration. Long story short, we decided that our dean was a dick, so we stuck twenty massive silicone dildos to his office door. Twenty extra-large, realistic dong and balls for every time he reprimanded us with detention or suspension. It's still a mystery how he found out that Olivia and I were behind the suction cupped sex toys. Our nine or ten months of proudly being juvenile delinquents came to an abrupt end when we tried to bust out of jail for my upcoming birthday. The release of repeat offenders who were still subject to strict supervision didn't exactly allow for extravagant birthday plans. Good behavior didn't even get us to the mall; our ankle monitors, also known as our mothers, only allowed for a boring ass sleepover. My partner in crime and I had no choice but to agree to the terms of our house arrest. But we could have celebrated in an old dirty box and made it extravagant; that's just what unicorns in a world filled with donkeys did—we made shit great.

On the eve of May 3rd, the night before my seventeenth birthday, my small party for two was crashed and ruined by a single boy. And when I say a single boy, I mean a thirty-year-old man-child who still lived at home, thus resulting in his lack of companionship. No woman wanted a man who catered to his mother for the mere payment of Cheetos and PlayStation.

"What are you jive turkeys doing?" My flunky brother Anthony busted in my room and scared the shit out of us. He was embarrassingly stuck in the seventies; the way he spoke and his style was stolen straight from the disco era, which was absurd for someone who was born in the eighties. Olivia and I marveled in remarkable retro throwbacks in music, movies and moguls before our time, but you wouldn't catch us with R&B finger-waves or Bill Cosby sweaters. I wished my brother admired from afar like us. A jheri-curl and fanny pack, I could have possibly stomached, but not the patterned polyester rags that clung unhealthily tight to his body parts and certainly not the pointy collared shirts that he left open at the chest.

"Leave us alone and go choke on your malt liquor, you loser." My love for him was tolerant at best. Our sibling rivalry ran rampant with disrespect, pranks, and frustration for our mother—it was a normal brother and sister relationship.

"Just making sure there ain't no suckas hiding out in here, ya dig? You're both far too young to be giving up the trim." Anthony stood in the doorway filling his body with Colt 45. I annoyingly stared at him pondering his existence.

"Can we have some of your beer?" Olivia questioned him. My annoying stare turned towards her.

Anthony thought about it for a second and agreed, "Right on, young bucks…meet me in the kitchen."

"What's wrong with you? He'll rat us out to Sophie."

"Then we'll rat him out for enabling underage drinking. Come on, this party needs a little party." Olivia grabbed my hand and pulled me in the direction of trouble. Anthony was dropping ice cubes into two glasses when we entered the kitchen.

"Beer is better cold. Here you are you, groovy ladies. Bottoms up!" I didn't trust my brother's deceitful ass, but he did always seem to give me a pass for my birthday. One day free of torture was the only gift I looked forward to. The three of us raised our beers and clinked glasses.

"Cheers." We immediately spewed the fermented brew from our mouths. Our bitter beer faces grossly turned into we-just-swallowed-Anthony's-piss faces.

"What the fuck is wrong with you?!" I was disgusted.

"Hey, watch your mouth?" My archrival had the nerve to police my profanity after he just served us fluid that was stored in his bladder and discharged through his penis. Yuck!

"Are you serious?!"

"I'm dead serious ,and that'll teach you girls to stay away from alcohol."

"The only thing you taught us is that you don't drink enough water. News flash, it's 2013 and disco is dead you fucking idiot!" We ran from the kitchen.

"No need to get nasty, but let me know when you want to tell Mom. She'd love my side of the story." Anthony antagonized me with this brown, glue-like Chapstick that kept his lips puckered to our mother's ass. Telling Sophie what had occurred was pointless; Anthony was her golden shower child.

After we drowned our tongues in bleach and mouthwash, we eventually settled down.

"I'm gonna say it now, in case I don't make it to midnight…happy crawled-out-the-cooch day, best friend." Olivia wanted to be the first to wish me love and all the desires of my heart on the anniversary of my birth. She was also the first to fall asleep, permitting me to talk to my other bff: myself. I read once that talking to oneself didn't make a person crazy, but a proven genius. Vocal clarification and validation was important.

"I'm going to have a great birthday," I whispered to myself as I rested my eyes and prayed to the birthday gods for the desires of my heart. Now, usually I prayed for world peace, tickets to Ellen's 12 Days of Giveaways show, and pretty rainbows that led to pots of gold so I could afford to move out of Sophie's house, but that night, I put my trivial requests on hold and begged for an adventurous surprise. My special day only came around once a year, and I reserved the right to have the day be all about me. My plea was absolutely selfish and so what? My life was about as exciting as Toddlers & Tiaras, before Honey Boo Boo came on the scene. I wanted similar, accidental beauty queen fame, even if only for a day. I closed my eyes with great expectation and fell asleep.

The healthy concoction of junk food and sugary liquids produced quite the terrifying fantasies while our adolescent bodies rested. Whereas Olivia dreamt of a twerking Cinderella, my mental images weren't so Disney Gone Wild. My brain activity was intense to say the least and my so-called dream resembled a wicked thriller. It was so vivid. I woke up just after midnight and slowly gravitated towards Olivia. I slowly crawled over the blankets and pillows that formed a pallet on my bedroom floor and I straddled her body. My actions were involuntary and scared me—I wanted to wake up and regain control. I vaguely remember my mother's warning that eating crap before going to sleep caused bad dreams, but damn, what the hell did I eat—a chocolate covered zombie?! I hovered over my best friend, drawing her in at an unforgiving force, literally sucking the life out of her. The pressing of my lips against hers was an awkward exchange, especially since she was like a sister to me (and I had already arranged my marriage with Bruno Mars, as soon as he realized I existed). I'd seen people kissing each other before, but neither one seemed to be in such physical terror. Clearly it wasn't a transfer of affection as her eyes popped opened in fear. I had interrupted her animated illusions and pulled her into my nightmare. My rapid suction reduced air pressure from her lungs and I inhaled her entire being to the point that her shoulders and neck raised from the ground.

"Chance!" My mother's voice disconnected the iridescent air flow between us. I'm sure she didn't expect her nightly check of two teenage girls to reveal something sinister. It wasn't until I witnessed Olivia limp and lifeless that I realized I was wide awake. I didn't need to be pinched; I was absolutely conscious and coherent when my mother shoved me out of the way. It was no dream. Sophie pushed me and I scurried to the closest corner. Sweat beads of anxious perspiration roofed my entire head and the extreme heat formed and dripped south. The commotion on the inside of my skull was far more severe; each indecisive thought stabbed my brain with needles. Aches in my heart made their debut: an attack.

"Come on Oliva, wake up honey," Sophie frantically whimpered. I watched in guiltiness as my mother smacked her cheeks and began resuscitation. Remorse held my eyes open wide, frozen stiff.

"What did you do to her?" She tried to get an understanding. I asked myself the same question a thousand times in the few minutes that moved in slow motion. I provided no answers, nor any solutions. The room soon crowded with my brother whom ran to my mother's cries. The palms of Anthony's hands pushed into Olivia's chest, while my mom pushed breath into her lungs. Their rescue attempts failed; there was no sign of life. I believed Olivia was dead.

"Call 911!" Normally when you accidentally take your friend's life, you stay around and explain how you woke up and found her unresponsive and immediately attempted CPR. Unfortunately for me, all the notes I'd taken while watching Snapped, Dateline, and How To Get Away With Murder were useless, seeing as though I was caught in the act. And I conveniently forgot to ask my mom if she'd ever lie for me in the event I needed a corroborating alibi. Whenever the shock of the terrifying occurrence subsided, I intended to run. But for the moment, all I could do was drown in the downpour of chaotic tears, not just from my eyes, but every living panicked set of eyes in the room.

"I think she's dead." The disappointment in my mother's voice and the hopelessness on her face, as if she were cradling her own dead child, released my muteness and moved my shocked body.

"I'm sorry," I expressed shame and ran like hell. Killing my best friend wasn't exactly how I intended to kick off my adventurous birthday.

"Chance!" Anthony authoritatively yelled at my back. Turning my back on my best friend was so much more than teenage cattiness: this was betrayal. This was murder. While most asked Jesus what he would do in problematic circumstances, I turned to more tangible icons, real or otherwise, for guidance to act in a manner that would demonstrate a favorable outcome for myself. The navigation of my moral compass might have been broken, only pointing in a selfish direction. Relatable scenarios shuffled through my mind before settling on a mentor; what would Tupac do? In his role as Bishop in the movie Juice, right after he killed his friend, he ran…and so did I.

My heart raced just as fast as my bare feet, but the adrenaline didn't take me far. I felt weak. Maybe the act of treachery had gotten the best of me. I stumbled across the street and eventually fell amongst the bushes of a nearby house. I guess it was a good place to hide since my pained legs were leaving me no other choice. Sweat dripped from every gland while my skin itched uncontrollably. How the hell did I manage to find a poison ivy burning bush? God was punishing me. My instant failing health took a backseat to the death that replayed in my head like ESPN highlights, but something was definitely wrong with me though. I pushed the poisonous leaves from my view in an attempt to survey my surroundings and awaited any activity from my house. I waited for sound, like a screaming ambulance, or even Olivia's screaming parents emerging from their speeding car and violently entering my front door in search of their daughter's remains. My stakeout came to an abrupt end when the unpleasant sensation of blurred vision, dizziness, and ultimately unconsciousness happened.

# kiss of death

You know those peaceful mornings when you awake to singing birds wishing you a good day with harmonic adoration—well on this morning, that songbird didn't feel like harmonizing. Instead it ingested bath salts and viciously pecked at my worm like toes that stuck out beyond the bushes. Frightened, I kicked and took a second to grasp the reality of why I was one with nature or possibly on an episode of Naked and Afraid.

"It wasn't a dream." I played back the events that brought me to my current state of vagrancy. Normally our neighbor's un-manicured yard was an eyesore, but that day, my disheveled self fit right in. I pulled my knees to my chest to mask my exposed limbs and continued my surveillance from the night before. Not much had changed since I passed out; if anything, my extreme fatigue and bruised skin had gotten worse, but my block was noiseless. And if there was any further commotion at my house, I obviously missed it. I didn't have to sit with leaves pricking my ass for long; shortness of breath and a nosebleed brought me to the surface to seek help. I fainted in the middle of the street.

Opening my eyes and finding myself in foreign environments had become a habit. I woke to discover that I had been placed on a stiff cot with adjustable side rails. I'm not sure how exactly I arrived in a hospital, but I must admit it was better peeing in a bedpan than outside in the yard like a dog. Every inch of my skin felt like it was on fire from an apparent rash that changed the color and texture of my appearance—this was more than just an allergic reaction to some un-manicured shrubs. My joints were so swollen I could barely move to examine the IV stuck in my arm. I scanned the room to see if there was a nurse to tell me why my body had gone rogue, how long I had to live, and if she could kindly pass me my phone to update my Facebook status before I died. There was no nurse, but maybe a ghost.

"Olivia." Instantaneously, my eyes stretched wide, my eyebrows raised to the sky, and my heart thumped violently against my ribs. It was traumatizing to see

Olivia alive and casually slouched in a chair next to my bed texting.

"No…it's Britney, bitch," she joked, but I didn't laugh. My sense of humor was diluted by the seriousness of it all—although I didn't know what "it all" was. So, either I was being visited by the ghost of best friends past or this Britney girl was Olivia's doppelganger.

"You're alive?" I was confused.

"And so are you…I mean, you look like shit, but I'm glad to see you're awake. The doctor says you're not doing too well." She leaned in with fear.

"I'm not sure what happened last night, but I knew you wanted to secretly suck my face since the day we met, hoe. I support you, but you'll be swimming in that lady pond alone, Boo." We giggled. Though she made light of the unexplained situation, I was disturbed that we were in the Twilight Zone.

"Ms. Joseph, you should be back in your bed; you're still under observation." The doctor reprimanded Oliva for being outside of her own room.

"I feel great as a new born baby, Doc. Love you and see you later girl." Olivia gave me a hug goodbye and left my room. The cotton gown designed for easy access exposed her bare baby ass as she exited. Dr. Till wasted no time revealing the source of my agony; acute leukemia flooded the blood that flowed throughout my body. I had no idea what he was talking about.

"Oh my God, honey." My mother rushed to my bedside from the doorway where she appeared and calculatingly observed from afar—maybe fearful that I was contagious or possessed. I was unexpectedly happy to see her. And by happy to see her, I meant happy that she could decipher what this quack was rambling on about.

"How are you feeling? Where does it hurt? Have you eaten anything?" She went on and on just as any doting mother would. Eaten? I was dying, and she was curious about my last meal.

"Have we met?" I thought to myself. I didn't recognize this gentle woman making a loving fuss over me, suddenly and surprisingly overbearing. She was dangerously close, but made sure not to deface her Saks Fifth Avenue catalog outfit or exchange her Chanel perfume with my unpleasant stench of death. I couldn't remember the last time she even hugged me, and I wished she didn't pretend to do it at that moment either; her touch pained my flesh.

"Olivia's alive, Mom." I reassured her that I wasn't a killer.

"Yeah, she woke up not too long after you ran out. You're scaring me honey. What's going on with you?"

All it took was being on the verge of death to some-what reactivate her maternal attachment to me. Dr. Till politely asked her to get off my bed and he gently con-tinued with his diagnosis. I checked every symptom box he detailed of the cancer: joint pain, extreme fatigue, fever, bruising, pale skin, short of breath, confusion, and my hemoglobin levels were so low that it left me wide open for infection. As a result, I also had pneu-monia. The doctor was just full of good news—a ray of fucking sunshine. The disease had progressed to the point where my quality of life had rapidly diminished. I was beyond medication, I was beyond blood transfu-sions. I was beyond soothing my saddened mother who sobbed just enough to show that my pain provoked her. He prepared us for end of life as I closed my eyes for what felt like the last time. Well, it was the time before the last time.

"Chance!" Sophie screamed. Damn, she wouldn't let me live peaceful and passing on peacefully wasn't an option either. I couldn't even muster up the oomph to mouth a final "shut the fuck up" to her before I gave in and surrendered to my demise. I closed my eyes and everything went black.

Did I believe in miracles? Or, at the least, maybe mutants? Well I had to put my confidence in something:

magic, The Wizard of Oz, maybe Beetlejuice…Beetlejuice, Beetlejuice, Beetlejuice? Saying his name three times didn't summon the rowdy spirit of Michael Keaton because clearly, I didn't need him. Undoubtedly, I still resided in the land of the living. I felt great, whole again. No achy joints, no fever, no extreme pain or fatigue, and thank God, no phlegm, puss filled lungs. Visualize a squirrel, one minute all happy go lucky on an open highway to heaven and then, bam, flattened by an assassin semi-truck. The truck driver looks back and witnesses the squirrel flipping him the bird before it scurries off into the enchanted forest. That was me: resilient roadkill. I don't know how, but the restoration of the physical damage to my tissues and organs was repaired. Resumption of the normal functioning of my body was an understatement; I was healed. It was a situation not explicable by natural or scientific laws, but I damn sure wasn't concerned with questioning the phenomenon. I pulled the tubes connected to my body and jumped out of my death bed. Amazement was glued on my face as I examined my reflection in the tiny bathroom mirror. Everything was back to normal—well everything except small circular marks on each of my cheeks. It was odd, but I doubt anyone would come out of my similar misfortune of attempted murder, sleeping on the street, and dying from cancer with only a few scars. I was more than fucking grateful; the jolly twerk of my butt was proof. The opening of my hospital room door interrupted my thrusting hips. I recognized the uninvited guest from TV; it was Kitty Kate, a ruthless journalist whose stories were just as idiotic as her name. She excelled merely because most people had rather believed an outlandish lie than the dreary truths of our reality.

"I'm hoping we can get a quick interview with the miracle girl who was healed of cancer overnight." She barged in my room. Security dressed in scrubs rushed in after her.

"It's Sunday for goodness sake. Get your ass outta here and go interview Jesus at church. Chick-fil-A, Chick-fil-A!" She vehemently moonwalked the reporter's feet backwards out of my room and slammed the door.

"Chick-fil-A?" I was confused.

"Yeah you know, closed on Sundays. And I'm sure there will be more reporters and cameramen just like them nosey bastards." My feisty nurse lowered the blinds to the window that allowed full on peepage of my room.

"I already know it was blabber mouth Martha who called the paparazzi. She has HPV mouth."

"HPV?" I had no clue what language this lady was speaking.

"Yeah you know, stuff flows outta her mouth like a heavy period vagina. Unfortunately, it's not just once a month, it's every fucking day! Oh, excuse my language, honey. I'm Lisa and I've been watching over you since you got here. If I hadn't treated you myself, I would never believe what I'm witnessing right now. Shit, I must have the Midas touch." Lisa was bluntly entertaining while she routinely monitored my temperature, pulse rate, blood pressure, and patted herself on the back.

"You're perfect honey. I'll get the orderlies to bring you some food, and not that mush that tastes like we stole it from a doggy bowl, but the good stuff that the cooks make for me and my two big friends. She placed her hands on her chest and perked up her boobs on the way out. Two big boobs left and one big boob entered.

"I knew you'd come around. Come here, let me see you." Sophie obsessed over me. She licked her thumb and tried to smudge away the new scars on my face. The smell of ancient, funky coffee made me sick again. I couldn't even pick my nose without her wanting to examine the gold I'd found in it. She coddled me through final tests, discharge, and into the car. It was annoying, but I milked every bit of it as she pushed the wheelchair, that I didn't need, down the hospital halls. I caught HPV mouth Martha tryna snap a pic of me on her phone on our way out. I gave her the best angle of my middle finger scratching my forehead. We were met at the entrance of the hospital by my Driving Miss Daisy looking ass brother. His contaminated piss probably had something to do with my fleeting terminal illness. I'd deal with him later. Once inside of the black Navigator, Sophie's warm gentle care turned ice, ice cold. Without the audience or debilitating disease, Cruella de Vil was back to her old self.

"What's this for?" I questioned Sophie after she handed me a stack of stapled papers.

"I paid thousands of dollars for your private education; the least you can do is pretend to know how to read." I read what I could of the simple black text; the contents were perplexing. There was a name I could barely pronounce: Dr. Dietrich Anschuetz, and a shit load of questions pertaining to the functioning of my organs.

"He's a renowned doctor who researches cases like yours. What if this craziness happens again? He needs to know about you before your appointment with him in a few weeks—he'll be flying out from Germany to examine you."

"You want me to willingly give my body to some German Nazi scientist? No way. I'm no longer a case. I'm healed. I can't even understand half of this anyway."

"You will fill it out, and Anthony will be thrilled to sign you up for German lessons, so you can better understand it or you can Google it like all the other lazy millennials." There were so many things wrong with Sophie's commands. First off, German? I had barely mastered the foreign language of English. Second, I'd rather Anthony order the Spanish edition of Rosetta Stone so I could translate all the shit my nail lady talked about me. And third, I refused to freely offer up specimen of my brain for the second coming of Holocaust experiments that resulted in disfigurement and death—no thank you. This doctor may have shared the same motives as that Kitty cartoon reporter, or worse. Money must have been on the table, and just how much was Sophie going to get for pimping out her only daughter anyway? Next she'd book me on the Dr. Oz show, and then have me selling flat tummy tea on the 'gram. There was no telling with my mother. I feared her wrath, so I later found an online English to German translator and filled in the complicated questionnaire with lyrics to Jingle Bells. Christmas could put the Grinch in a good mood. The rest of our car ride home was quiet until I caught Anthony's creepy eyes staring at me through the rearview mirror.

"What'd the doctors say was wrong with her?" Anthony, as well as myself, was interested in the expert's answers. We both looked to Sophie in the passenger's seat.

"Whatever she had resembled something called empathic illness where you take on symptoms of others who are sick. It's not so much physical as it is psychological." Sophie basically made me sound insane, like it was all in my head. Her theory may have rung true if I were actually around someone who was sick.

"You ain't gotta be a doctor to see the girl is a psycho. I think her and Olivia had a bad trip on some drugs, if you ask me." Anthony's response made my eyes roll. Of course the bootlicker had shit on his tongue, and undoubtedly those drugs he spoke of came from his system. I was not some crackhead mental case as they described me. The only good thing about being part of a dysfunctional family was at least they bad mouthed me to my face. I remained inaudible for the rest of the ride.

The whirlwind that was my life had blown me right back where I began: back in my room cursing out the birthday gods for giving me exactly what I wished for. How dare they. Once the dust had settled, and my mother gave up on donating my body for research, I was still left with misery. I much rather preferred being pimped out by my mother to a Nazi doctor, than I did having her as a teacher. Apparently I was under review with the school board, thus resulting in torturous home schooling to finish out the semester. My homeschool curriculum resembled the dreadful tasks of a personal assistant, not a student. I'd be woken up at 5 a.m., given two hours to finish my school work with no instruction, an hour or so to complete a list of chores, and the rest of the day was dedicated to making calls, scheduling appointments, drafting e-mails and organizing files. My new "teacher" claimed it was the life skills training that was most beneficial and necessary for a young girl's life. Life skills training my ass—it was a violation of the child labor laws. According to the federal rules and regulations, I was working in hazardous conditions: knee deep in Sophie's bullshit. Not to mention my educational opportunities were in jeopardy, due to the fact that my high school graduation was just a month away. I should have been focused on my required coursework and final tests. I desired a diploma, not the hard knock life fuckery. I allowed my mind to stray from my oh-so-trivial problematic life. It wandered to a few old raggedy boxes that were shoved in the back of Sophie's closet. I hung my mother's dry cleaning and pushed the hangers aside for full access. I peeled open the flaps of the first box and shuffled through real estate documents of her many investments. A thick folder labeled with my brother's name would hopefully give me ammo to use against him in our next battle.

"Get the hell out of my things!" Sophie was a tyrant. Damn, just when I'd found something possibly salacious, here comes soggy Sophie. My existence officially sucked balls. Ninety percent of my misery derived from separation anxiety—I missed my cotton candy unicorn so I decided to reach out—again.

"How are you feeling? I think Anthony contaminated us with his pissticide! lol. I'm sorry for all the craziness. I still don't know what happened. Miss you." I texted Olivia. Up until that point, all of my communications had gone unanswered. But this time she answered.

"Hey girl! My mom has been monitoring my phone. Not talking to you has been torment. Oh shit, here she comes. Hope to see you at graduation! Love you." Her response was short, but effective to my soul. I couldn't wait until graduation.

Shockingly, I endured all of Sophie's bitchy antics right up to the big day without any hostile reactions on my end. I was a model citizen and ready to be reunited with my best friend.

"Congratulations to the graduating class of 2013!" I believe our screams of celebration were a combination of the completion of school and the conclusion of all the boring ceremonial speeches. My classmates had to nudge me awake twice due to my hibernating snores. It must have been the nervous anticipation of the day's events that only afforded me three hours of restless sleep. I had hoped for a little more excitement, given we had to cut a deal to even be in the auditorium that day. Once the school caught wind of what happened, compliments of Olivia's mom, I was banned from campus after the board's review. I believe my dismissal letter stated something about child endangerment and being a risk to my peers—it was two pages of ambiguous crap because no one, not even me, could explain the true events of that night. But since they had already spent my mother's hefty donation check on bullshit bonuses and new faculty lounge, they at least agreed to allow me to walk with my class with security two steps behind. High school graduation should be a thrilling time with friends whom have endured the countless hours of mind-numbing education with you, but my unicorn was instructed to stay away from the troublemaking monster in the cap and gown. Our plans to confidently cross the stage feeling ourselves like Beyonce and Nicki with a final "fuck you" to the dean of students, in our eyes, were ruined. We never reunited in person that day, but cheered for each other when our names were announced.

"My mom is a protective cunt, sorry. Here's to our future!" She ended her text message with an emoji of two champagne glasses. I didn't hold the commands of Olivia's helicopter mom against my best friend. Most parents were oblivious to the idea that they could ever produce a hellion. Somewhere in the midst of Olivia's constant detentions, theft, and sexual explorations, I somehow became the bad influence. Receiving my diploma wasn't as gratifying as I imagined—I could have received it in the mail just the same. I felt empty just standing around watching my peers being celebrated and joyfully capturing their memories on their camera phones. But that soon changed when an unlikely person kindly approached me.

"Hey Chance, a few of us our going to bowl and eat pizza at Lucky's—wanna come?" Lauren Wells always extended me an invite to any and everything; she mostly asked me to go to the bathroom with her. And although constant group urination was suspect, I still thought of her as one of those genuinely nice, positive people. Considering we didn't have overactive bladders in common, I was surprised she wanted to hang where toilets weren't immediately present.

"I'll pee there…I mean, I'll be there! Thanks for the invite." Expectedly, Sophie didn't organize a celebratory dinner or get-together for my achievement, so I had no other obligations to break. My warden permitted a few hours to congregate—but not without my brother as a prison guard to enforce rules and control extreme situations. Anthony was a terrible choice given his attention span was about as long as his penis: a photographic fact I wished I could have aggressively scraped from my mind after an unfortunate bathroom encounter. I, of course, complied to her terms, knowing I'd have complete freedom to enjoy my time outside of my cell.

We finished our first official obligation in life, and subsequent to any accomplishment, a party was in order. Similar to the spectacular and prolific grand opening ceremonies of the Olympics, we too paraded into a sports arena in perfect synchronization to the harmonic beat of determination. In my mind, our entrance was super dramatic and in slow motion; in reality, we were just overdressed teens entering the bowling alley. The provoking aroma of funky feet and dirty ashtrays quickly penetrated our hair and clothes as we met our opponents. Ernest Harris and Malcom Johnson greeted us. Malcom was a sexy mixed mullet of Obama and Chris Brown: business in the front and party in the back. Class president and class clown made him exceedingly appealing and most likely to succeed with me. Calling him Obama Brown in passing was my corny way of flirting with him. He reciprocated by treating me like all the rest of his building relationships; he flashed his impeccable masculine smile, shook hands, and kissed the babies on their cheeks. Now normally, two varsity football players against two semi-intellectual girls would be deemed unfair, however, I'd watched endless hours of professional bowling and Happy Gilmore—mentally, all I needed was a members only jacket to play in a league. It was going to take me, Lauren, a prayer, and a box of Lucky Charms for this to be a fair matchup. With such cutthroat competition, we were overly determined to reign victorious, and when I say we, I meant me, since Lauren was in the bathroom. Typically, I was quietly laid back in most settings, but it was something about making the natural born athletes look bad, that I let loose an unrestrained impulse to talk shit and gun for the gold. Perhaps it was the spiked liquid courage we sipped from a plastic water bottle.

"You ready for this whoopin' we're 'bout to serve up?" I could taste victory on my trash talking tongue.

"Let's bowl!" My peeing partner declared with excitement.

By the tenth frame, Lauren's and mine combined score was pathetic, to say the least. The large amount of pizza and grape soda my teammate had consumed was weighing heavy on her bladder. She had flushed her competitive spirit down the toilet.

"Okay, it's time to focus girl. Keep your back straight and bend your knees. You're a cool chick, but I'll sit on your stomach if we lose," I whispered in Lauren's ear. I gave her an encouraging pat on the butt and pushed her towards the lane. Her Fred Flintstone twinkle toes were impressive; the gutter ball she tossed was not. Obama Brown was up next. With poise and expert stance, he took two smooth strides, swung and released the ball.

"Gutter ball!!!" I reported the play. Malcom was undoubtedly throwing the game, but I didn't care why because we were trailing by ten points. With the pressure left on my shoulders to come from behind and win, I rubbed my hands together in hopes of sparking some good luck. Using the dots as a guide, I lined up my feet, crystallized my thoughts, aimed for the pins, and prayed to sweet baby Jesus. The slow spin of the ball left me nervous as all hell. I closed my eyes and waited for the crash of the pins.

"Strike, strike, strike!" Lauren yelled with excitement behind me. My eyes peeled open to witness an empty lane. Before I could even turn around to boast, Malcom had met my lips with his. His intentions were revealed; letting us win was all a part of his plan. My bragging rights were denied, but the tingle that jam-packed my internal being was prize enough for me.

"We have to pee." I wasn't sure how else to maturely respond. I yanked Lauren by the hand and forced her into group urination.

"OMG was that your first kiss?" She asked with a fascinated concern and a Kool-Aid smile plastered on her face (grape flavored to be exact).

"Yeah. What happens next?"

"You go back out there, go with the flow, be yourself, and next time use your tongue." Usually I'd follow Olivia's reckless advice and end up in trouble, so with any luck, Lauren's guidance would prove the opposite. It was worth a shot—or at least another shot of whatever it was we were sipping from the water bottle. Lauren threw her head back and finished off the alcohol. She passed me a piece of gum. Her lack of peer pressure and promotion of fresh breath was comforting. We may have ran to the bathroom like little school girls, but we walked out like wanna-be women, rejoining our defeated opponents with new found confidence.

"Would the beautiful lady like to chat with me outside?" I casually followed his lead, but secretly hid a charge of flattery. Malcom held the door open for me and draped the concrete stairs with his blazer to protect my dress. I guess chivalry wasn't dead; he was just hiding out as a horny seventeen year old boy. I gave Malcom credit; he pretended to be interested in my plans after high school for about two minutes before he arrested my lips again. He respectfully kept his hands to himself, but the jabbing of his tongue in my mouth was so disrespectful. I wondered why they called it a French kiss; it felt more like a karate kiss. I fearlessly took control of our lip lock by overpoweringly straddling his lap. It was an odd display of forceful affection for someone who had just experienced her first kiss with a boy just twenty minutes earlier. I pinned his back against the descending stairs and seriously inhaled every ounce of his life. I hoarded a distinct impression of this exact same violent situation with Olivia. The familiarity of déjà vu was a phenomenon I wished I wasn't experiencing. The severe force pushed my hair into the air as if I were standing in front of a motorized fan. Our once mutual uncontaminated affection, rapidly evolved into assault. His eyes popped open in terror until his lifeless body sunk. My brother tackled me like a real life correctional officer neutralizing a physical altercation. He not only disconnected the lustrous air flow between Malcom and me, I believe he also dislocated his shoulder when we hit the ground. Maybe if he had actually tried out for wrestling, instead of just watching it on TV, he would have grasped the techniques needed to maintain superior position in a takedown.

"Yo, what the hell Chance?!" Anthony reprimanded me and rushed his injured shoulder over to Malcom to check for signs of life.

"What did you do to him?" I heard that distraught tune before whcn Sophie grieved for Olivia; I was no longer a one hit wonder, but a repeat offender. His loud and spastic lecture fell on deaf ears; I was incompetent. Both of our coping mechanisms were fragmented.

"I...I don't know...I'm sorry." Repentance cried from my tongue. Arriving to this ill-fated moment proved to be miserable in comparison to what was a previously striking night; the celebration was over. My careless actions would undeniably hold repercussions that I could never clarify. I was beyond explanation. I ran the last time and my mind agreed to the same plan, but my weakened body thought it best I stay on the scene. I dropped to my knees and vomited before I blacked out.

The closest I'd been to an actual oxygen mask was twenty minutes into a four hour long flight when I suffered an anxiety attack due to extreme claustrophobia and nausea. I was the main ingredient in an oversized sandwich that smelled like dirty belly button and unsanitary sexual relations. There was an extremely overweight man to my left, an equally sized woman to my right and neither exercised their right to wear deodorant. The involuntary sensation to vomit was nearing, and my overreaction to the funky situation forced me to reach up and claw at the airplane compartment containing the oxygen masks above the row of our coach seats. I cried to the flight attendant who quickly released me from the hot garbage imprisonment and breathed first class life into my body. Well, today was a horrific replication: I possessed that same feeling of inner turmoil and gasping for renewed air—only, this experience didn't end with upgraded comfort and luxury ventilation. I'd take that fiery pit of ass over the rapid decaying of my own body any day. I was back in a familiar but dreaded place; the hospital.

"She's suffering from an advance case of lung cancer. Are you sure all her systems just advanced today?" The doctor reviewing my charts was perplexed.

"Yes, she's been extraordinarily healthy for a little more than a month now. Can you please do something to help her breathing?" Sophie spoke for me. To which the doctor tried to address my mother's fear; explaining that the scary sensation of not being able to breath was common and he would try to make me as comfortable as he conceivably could.

"Oh okay, so she's been previously diagnosed and has experienced symptoms before?" He thought maybe we didn't understand the question the first time he asked.

"No, not like this, she had leukemia."

"She had leukemia just a month ago?" The physician was more fascinated with the plausibility of one patient having two types of life-threatening cancers, than he was with actually saving my life. Sophie instructed him to contact Dr. Till, who had treated me previously, but the severity of my current complications needed to be addressed instantly. I lost consciousness. Before Sophie could wrap her hands around the sluggish doctor's neck, I was placed on a ventilator. Aided oxygen cleared the offensive obstruction. How the hell was I fortunate enough to hit the "you're gonna fucking die" lottery twice? I hoped I'd be lucky enough to survive this misfortune too.

I must have had a rabbit's foot stuck up my ass, cause somehow I made it through again.

"I should get paid double for nurturing your ass back to life again, girl. Granted I'm good at my job, but if I was this fucking good, I certainly wouldn't be changing bed pans. I'd be walking on warm Miami water giving out free lives like Oprah." Nurse Lisa was surprised, as I was too, at yet another phenomenon. The process of complete restoration occurred for the second time; I was cancer free. My body incubated and cured the disease by repairing my tissues, organs and biological system as a whole; all within the laps of a day. The unreal lucidity fell upon me – the first time was a fluke, the second time was purposeful, and in the future…would it keep happening? The capability of possessing such an uncontrolled power was dangerous; it was a gift and a curse. Basically, I was fucked.

"You're fucked." Nurse Lisa shared my exact sentiments as she peeked beyond the blinds.

"I know an angel when I see one, but not everybody wears the same angelic glasses as I do. They wear the "I'm gonna run a bunch of test and dissect your ass" glasses. That's no way for you to live honey. Do you trust me?"

"I don't know."

"Of course you don't, and you can't trust the heart of every man. Two things to keep in mind: anyone who has ever declared that they know the cure for cancer has suddenly died and a man who leans to their own understanding will never allow an angel to spread their wings," Lisa shared her theories with conviction.

"So, what are you saying?"

"I'm telling you to do a damn makeup tutorial—girl, what the hell do you think I'm saying? You need to spread those wings of yours and get the hell out of here and fast. I'm supposed to alert the officers once you're conscious. I heard them talking to your mom about assault charges that were filed against you. I can't imagine you causing anyone harm honey." Nurse Lisa's eyes were sincerely concerned; wanting to know why she was about to make up a story of how I vanished into thin air. I told her what I knew.

"You're gonna think I'm Charlie Sheen cray, and according to Ancestry.com we're actually .002% related on my dad's side, so please give me the benefit of the doubt considering my bloodline. I seem to be attacking people, but in a good way. I forcefully vacuum nastiness from their mouths, take on their illness on a magnified level, and then it evaporates—poof I'm healed. It's the only way to explain it and I have no clue how or why." I didn't even believe me once I heard me say it aloud. I sounded absurd. She stared at me waiting for the part that was logical.

"I almost wished you hadn't told me—both our asses gonna be in a looney bin. Alright, no judgement. Just get dressed while I practice my performance." Nurse Lisa rehearsed her forged bewilderment for when the doctor, authorities, and my mother would noticed I was missing from my hospital bed. She even held her hand up to her forehead like a damsel in distress. She paused her dramatics to ask a personal question.

"Wait, can you take away my hemorrhoids?" I owed her one, but unfortunately only a high fiber diet and an enema could help her. Maybe a gift card to CVS Pharmacy and a *"I'm sorry about your hemorrhoids"* Hallmark Card could better articulate my gratitude. I got dressed and peeked beyond the door before running down the hospital's halls.

Slinking out of the building unobserved was fairly easy until I ran out the side door and right into that one reporter with the cracker jack name who busted in my room a month earlier.

"Oh shit. It's the miracle girl. I got a tip that you were diagnosed with yet another life-threatening cancer, but you look pretty alive to me. Are you gonna give me an exclusive revealing your secret, or should I just make it my life's mission to single white female your ass?" The grimy journalist tossed her cigarette and incredibly opened and pressed the red record button on her iPhone voice memos app within seconds. She was a pro.

"Ok sure. I have a mysterious ability to detect infections, and you my dear have contracted HPV from Martha's messy ass...oh, and it looks like syphilis as well. And yes you can quote me on that!" I continued my jailbreak from the hospital grounds with my middle fingers in the air. Squealing tires in the parking lot halted my escape yet again. The black van stopped right in front of me. It didn't match the silver Nissan Altima on my Uber app that was one minute away, so I apprehensively walked towards the rear of it. Although I couldn't see anyone behind the illegal tint, I felt creepy eyes follow me. I looked back, but no one got out the executive vehicle with no plates—maybe I was just being unreasonably suspicious, since hospital security would soon come after me. I jumped in my Uber and continuously checked the back window to make sure we weren't followed.

# fly the coop

I needed untraceable getaway transportation and the old rusted tricycle in the garage just wouldn't be fast and furious enough, should I be chased by anything other than an elderly cop with a walker.

"I wonder if I can fly." It was a reasonable question given my newfound capabilities. I foolishly flapped my arms in the air. What the hell was I thinking? I wasn't fucking Peter Pan—shit, I wasn't even athletic. If anything, my body was simply possessed.

"Focus, Chance." I hadn't planned on including anyone in my plot of escape, but I was left with no other choice than to add a Thelma to my Louise.

"I know your mom has a restraining order on me, but I need you to steal her car and help me run away."

It only took a second to receive a response to my text message.

"Say no more!" Clearly, Olivia had been waiting to be an accomplice to a crime. She was all too eager to add grand theft auto to her college applications. And just as promised, her enthusiasm journeyed intensely towards my house, hurling her mother's brand new Mercedes Benz into our driveway. Well, I assumed she was aiming for the designated pavement, even though she collided with the curb and our mailbox. Inexperience was an understatement—Olivia was only an hour into her thirty-hour driver's education course. I don't know if I was more afraid of potentially being an extraterrestrial being, or riding in the car with an unlicensed Uber driver on crack. Against my better judgement, I jumped in the car.

"What the hell, you're about as inconspicuous as a burglar going live on Facebook." I irritably admired the luxury landscaping job we left behind. Good thing I was running away, otherwise Sophie would kill me.

"Oh chill out. Now why am I voluntarily signing up for juvy? Where are we going?" Olivia mistakenly made herself more important in this here prison escape than needed. She was just a ride and possible ATM.

"It happened again." My enlightenment started slow inside our race car.

"You had another lesbian eruption?! I totally support your sexual orientation; you just gotta be a little more gentle, speaking from experience of course." My partiality to an innie or an outie was furthest from my mind. I needed to steer Olivia's mind and car out of the gutter. I found myself phantom steering the wheels from the passenger's seat.

"I kissed Malcom Johnson—but I didn't just kiss him, I sucked the life out of him, like I did with you." I elaborated a bit more and gave the same miniature testimony I shared with my Academy Award- winning nurse. Olivia periodically took her eyes off the road to inquisitively glance in my direction. A true friend knows your weaknesses, but will be your strength, and they'll feel your fears, but replenish your confidence. Olivia was obviously distracted and did neither.

"Did you always have those or are you doing that new faux freckle makeup trend?" Her focal interest made my eyes roll. A makeup tutorial was not forthcoming, but maybe a critical slap to convey the severity was in order. A tornado ripped through my life and whisked me into some alternate supernatural universe, and this hoe thought we were heading to see the wizard of cosmetics at Sephora.

"Have you ever been diagnosed with Leukemia?"

"Leukemia? What are you talking about girl?" Either she didn't know she was sick, or she wasn't and I somehow made the whole Freaky Friday thing up in my mind.

"Nevermind. Some serious shit is going on with me. I'm scared, and I just need you to drop me off in Mississippi or bumfuck Egypt—I don't know, whichever one we get to first." Wherever the yellow shit road would lead me.

"No fucking way. You don't have to run away, we can figure this shit out together. We're about to start college. You can't leave me." We sounded like a corny after school special.

"We've seen Powder and The Green Mile. You already know this will not end well for me. Hopefully I'll figure this out, get my life together, and be able to return soon. I just need you to help me with this, please." Mapquest guided our two-and-a-half hour road trip, and we formulated a terrible plan of action along the way. Well, at that time we didn't foresee the hot fiery mess that was to come; we naively lit a match with each idea. Stealing a car and fleeing the state was the first mistake—deciding to fake my death was even stupider. It was emphatically clear that all decisions thereafter helped spiral me into the depths of abyss.

"Let's simplify this. I'll post that I ran away on Facebook—if it's on the internet everyone will believe it. Then I'll ditch my phone and live off the grid. That way, I'll be untraceable. I'll slide through your DM, when I can, to keep in touch, and to beg for money of course." I picked up my phone and put my plan into action.

*"You may hate me but it ain't no lie*
*Baby bye bye bye*
*Bye bye*
*Don't want to make it tough*
*I just want to tell you that I've had enough*
*It might sound crazy but it ain't no lie*
*Baby bye bye bye."*

I updated my status with modified iconic NSYNC lyrics. For some reason the cryptic post just felt right. I transformed from a white boyband to an anxious googler. While Olivia shared her infinite wisdom of the world and rambled on about the pros and cons of traveling prostitution, I looked up the definition of cancer and how many different types there were. If my theory of an abysmal yeast-infected life was accurate, then I should know what I was up against. Cancer is the uncontrolled growth of abnormal cells, which can potentially invade other parts of the body and feast like the Last Supper. The cells may form a mass of tissue called a tumor. Cancers originate in a certain body part, and that body part may contain multiple types of tissues, so the disease can be categorized by the part of body or the cell; thus, resulting in over a hundred different known cancers that plague the human race. The physical impact was fatigue, pain, nausea, depression, loss in appetite, sleep deprivation, emotional distress—the list went on and on. I preferred to be a statistic of teenage pregnancy, if I had a choice. The interference of Olivia's tone-deaf harmony with Rihanna on the radio, and the ten unanswered text messages and calls from her mother, moved me to suggest a pit stop. I directed us off course to the nearest gas station when my own phone chimed in.

"Nosey cunt!" I reacted outloud to one of the new notifications.

"Yeah, my mom is a nosey cunt!"

"Yeah, moms are supposed to be, but I'm talking about Kitty Cunt Kate, that bitchy reporter." Just that quick, she had found my Facebook page and messaged me the title of her next story: Chance Dubois has Your

Cure for Cancer. She was infuriatingly relentless. I deleted and blocked her from my already private page. Fighting or folding to threats of compromising information was not on my list of things to do that day. Olivia pulled into the gas stations parking lot.

"So, how much money do you have on you?" It was time to ante up. My funds coupled with the stash stuck behind my brother's John Shaft picture frame summed about six hundred dollars. Anything Olivia could offer, would help.

"Umm…I have about two hundred in cash and my credit cards." Olivia pulled her contribution from her wallet.

"I need to borrow 170 of that. Use the thirty to fill up your mom's tank, and head back home." I decided that the random truck stop gas station was where me and Olivia would part ways.

"What? No. We're not even half way there." Dragging her into my shit would only add twice as many flies on this already steaming pile of shit. From that moment on, it was going to be a solo undertaking, and the only proof of our Ferris Bueller escapade would be the added miles to her car. I hoped they would go unnoticed too. We spent time laughing, crying, singing, talking shit, and grudgingly saying goodbye. When you create an alternate universe that revolves around someone, it's impossible to fathom an incredible future without them.

"Promise me you'll come back?" I promised her and prayed the time and space between us was not permanent. I got out of the car and watched her reluctantly drive away.

My only means of transportation to the next state would be gained by asking strangers for rides. It was known as hitchhiking, but also depicted as a sketchy invitation of death from every movie I had ever watched. Thumbing it was a crap shoot; you could get a Good Samaritan with compassion for your circumstances, or you could get a preying jackass with passion for your tits and ass. A free ride didn't always mean free, so I scouted the vehicles and their owners carefully. All pop-bellied bearded men were out; I had no desire to sit on Santa's lap. The stoic looking young couple in polos and patterned pants were truly, disgustingly dirty, searching for a sex slave to tie up in the basement. But the systematic single mother and her teenage son were the condom I'd needed; they were safe. I asked for a ride and they selflessly agreed.

"Thanks for helping me get to Mississippi. It's hard navigating through this thing called life without a helping hand." Although they gave the impression of normalcy, riding in a stranger's car was just awkward as hell. I showed appreciation nonetheless and mostly sat in the backseat in silence as they sang an hour's worth of their Taylor Swift favorites. Margaret steered the wheel and her evil cat road shotgun, while her son Ryan and I sat in the back. He periodically glanced my way then quickly looked away whenever I moved. Ryan seemed to lack social skills. Margaret, on the other hand, wouldn't shut the hell up. They were traveling from Texas to their cousin's farm to pick up three chickens and a pig, but their trip was prolonged due to the constant changing of her depends. Maybe I'd jump off their Noah's Ark at the next stop before it filled up with animals and urine—or sooner.

"So, are you a virgin? I only ask cause you're about my son's age, and he's never wet his whistle, if you know what I'm saying." Margaret's rearview mirror eyes went from Carol Brady to Kris Jenner, when she saw an opportunity for her son. If I didn't know any better, I'd say that I was in a stranger danger scenario—and outnumbered two to one.

"I can give you fifty bucks for the lift." The plan was to play the "I'm broke" role to preserve my funds, but I was willing to buy my way out of sexual assault. Unfortunately, Margaret locked all the doors from the front;

my money was no good in their establishment. The child safety locks built into rear doors to prevent unauthorized exit from the car rendered my door handle useless. How ironic that the damn safety lock wouldn't in fact keep me safe. I didn't panic. I had a new gift that could be used to my advantage. I played along.

"Okay. Gotta use what I got to get what I want, right?" I was finally able to use a Ronnie Hoe quote in real life; The Players Club wasn't just a guide for single mothers paying their way through college—it was also enlightening for my current unsolicited proposition. Margaret so graciously pulled over and got out the car to give us privacy; she wasn't a total sicko.

"Take your pants off." Ryan didn't sound all that inexperienced. It was obvious they had previously taken this show on the road.

"I don't work that fast, cowboy." I inelegantly turned his lap into a chair and dryly pecked his lips. I wasn't sure how to turn it on, but it needed to happen fast, before his clammy hands copped a meaningful feel. If I couldn't get it to work and render him lifeless, I'd be fucked, literally and figuratively.

"How's that feel? You like that?" I finally got it to work. I aggressively shoved two small dart-like electrodes into Ryan's dick; the electroshock disrupted his muscles and caused incapacitation. The taser delivered extreme pain and more importantly, compliance. It was the best going away gift Olivia could have ever given me. If Margaret were to peek in on us, it would appear that her precious son was suffering the biggest climax of his life. Disabling Ryan didn't disable the locked back-seat doors. I rolled down the window, reached for the outside handle, opened the door, and soundlessly met Margaret who sat on the front hood of the Pontiac.

"You're next, Momma Madam." I shocked his sadistic mother right in her vagina; it brought her to her knees. The sight of the predators through the vehicle's rear windshield was satisfying. I gave them my original offer of fifty bucks in exchange for a ride to Mississippi; it was so nice of them to allow me to drive there alone while they continued their perverted journey on foot. I ditched their car as soon as I saw civilization just beyond the state line. I was confident the reported stolen vehicle would eventually attract one Mississippi, two Mississippi, three Mississippi cops.

# not so super superhero

While I often subscribed to the notion that I knew it all, I didn't believe there was anyone with experience or a practical understanding of what I was going through; but I had to launch an investigation nonetheless. My optimistic attitude led me to seek professional advice from a doctor. I entered the community facility with my curls tucked away and my low head strongly protected by my hooded sweatshirt, suspicious of my surroundings and even more fearful that someone would recognize my face from a news report on TV or any social media outlet offered. I just knew Sophie had an APB out on me by now. With random nosey eyes questioning my anonymous presence, I suddenly wished the world would regress back to the olden times when current events were only spread through bored housewives and delayed printed publications—you know B.C., before Chance. My notoriety was most likely all in my head and the people were looking past my paranoid ass. I sat down amongst the crowd and chewed my paranoid fingernails, probably inadvertently gnawing on nasty door handle disease, before I placed them on the keyboard and typed WebMD into the internet browser of the library's computer. I thought a clinic of knowledge was a lot safer than an actual infested free clinic. My electronic physician asked for a list of my symptoms, but I was hesitant. How could I anticipate a real diagnosis when I couldn't even sanely articulate my condition? The drop-down options didn't quite capture my psychopathic episodes, so I skipped over all the unrelated bullshit and entered a transparent synopsis: involuntarily sucking the life out of humans. With all seriousness, I characterized myself as a vacuum vampire. Although I was embarrassed and questioned my mental stability, I submitted my answer anyhow. And I can't say I was shocked by the suggested treatment: "Immediately dial 911." I was tempted to suck the life out of the damn computer. I needed help damnit!

The internet couldn't tell me who or what I morphed into, but it could surely tell me who was concerned for the old me: the me about a week ago. Our nation had come a long way from missing children appearing on the sides of milk cartons, and for good reason—what if the one person who could save my life was lactose intolerant? The average person spent about two hours a day on social media; technology has made it conceivable to reach the masses. On the flip side, it has also invited the masses of pervs and murderers to reach their victims virtually. My motives weighed more on the narcissistic side as I logged into my Facebook account. I clicked cautiously through my notifications, which were appallingly few. I received three likes on my last cryptic runaway post and one comment: "Home Alone is a classic! Did you see the sequel?" What kind of dumb ass question was that? Of course I saw the second one. Why hadn't anyone taken my post seriously? I'd been gone for two days. Why wasn't anyone checking for me? Maybe I'd left an impression in another place. Chance Dubois of New Orleans. It wasn't the first time I googled myself, but it was the first time my search generated anything that could hinder my chances of becoming Miss America. I was a missing person, but with a warrant out for my arrest for the assault of Malcom Johnson. I gave Obama Brown the best lip lust of my life while simultaneously saving his life, and this was the fucking thanks I got.

"Shit!" The internet was an enlightening and completely traceable informant. I deleted my search history and wiped the keys and mouse clean. I left the computer station and headed for the literature.

I was physically engulfed in a wealth of knowledge and, of course, the first thing that came to mind was X-Men. I actually wasted an hour of my life flipping through the pages and there was no comic book character I even closely resembled. Clearly, I was the bootleg version of a hero and a villain—all unenthusiastically smashed together like Ellen Degeneres and Donald Trump. The equivalent of a gift and a curse. The foundation of the Marvel crusaders guided me to a more realistic section of the library: biology. A mutant arises from a genetic evolution. If I could just understand the effect the mutation in my genes had on the sequence change within my DNA, maybe I could reverse the diabolical organism taking over my body, and solve world fucking peace. I had no clue what the hell I was reading—I only passed biology because I spelled my name correctly, and the teacher couldn't take another semester of me and Olivia. I probably had more luck looking at all the pretty pictures of the comic books, than I did comprehending the interworking of my body. I was getting nowhere. If knowledge was power, I was about as strong as Elmer's Glue on a broken bone. The ability to sustain my attention on a single topic was crucial, yet I found myself distractingly fascinated by fashion magazines—borrowing fabric patterns and accessories to mentally construct my costume. All the notable superheroes hid their identity, while also wanting to be uniquely identified by tight-ass jazzy, indestructible materials. But since I didn't have access to similar chic superhuman resources, good thing I already wore a permanent disguise: freckles were beginning to mask my face. I just couldn't make the correlation between the tiny scars appearing with each cancer I eliminated.

"Focus, Chance." I'd stacked so many books and magazines around me, I had built a scholar mess. Something amongst the pages had to hold some bold, significant importance. And there it was, just below an envious photo of Jessica Alba on the cover of a Women's Health magazine: The Statistics of Cancer. I inquisitively spun to the twenty-third page and read over the article. The statistics at a glance were a massive burden on the human race. Almost forty percent of men and women would be diagnosed with cancer at some point in their life. An estimated number of diagnoses in children in a single year exceeded fifteen thousand. New cancer cases would rise over twenty million over the next few decades, and cancer was among the leading cause of death worldwide. Everyday evils of murderers and rapists never closely concerned me—well, besides my monstrous mother—but now I was personally inundated with the most sinister device of all. It festered inside of me like so many other innocent people. I joined the statistic figures of those affected by the deadly disease and added one of my own: assessed number of women who can single handedly decrease incidence and mortality of cancer was one. Why was this happening to me?

"Motherfuck cancer!" The inability to change my circumstances furiously spewed from my mouth. I sounded like Samuel Jackson in every movie role he'd ever played.

"Yeah, fuck cancer!" some random guy nearby concurred. The support was widespread and proved that everyone was only a molecule away from a cancerous cell, whether it be in them or in someone sitting next to them.

"Shhhh!" The loud shushing librarian was clearly against the fight. She must have had allies with the pharmaceutical industry who possessed the cure, but had no intentions of sharing it.

The vibrations of a severely obstructed airway raised my head from a book. She snored like a man three times her size, but more importantly, an unsupervised cellphone balanced on her hibernating, inflatable belly. It was a lifeline to phone a friend. How could I capitalize on the opportunity; should I have called Sophie to save me from my new life of poverty and thievery, or contacted Olivia for the warmth of familiarity? Outrageously, I chose sentimentality over the real thing—nostalgia over a warm meal and bed. Delusional despair had clearly taken over my rationality. I gently reached over and saved her phone from falling and cracking the screen. She was so careless like the people who fall asleep with a lit cigarette. Thank goodness I was there.

"Damn." No screen protector, but password protected. I quickly developed trust issues with her. The nerve of her to assume that someone would take her phone while she slept to make a free call. Her noisy breathing turned to high-pitched squealing.

"Security!" She woke up and snitched on me.

"No, no, wait. I'm sorry. I just need to call my family." I begged for sympathy, but sharing her unlimited minutes wasn't an option.

"Serves you right. You should have used the payphone." Now she was just being patronizing; payphones were a myth. I was escorted away from the stingy woman and right out the library doors. In an attempt to save face, I knocked over a stack of books on my way out.

I exited exactly how I entered; a homeless oblivious freak. Now what?

A heavily forested state with a population of approximately three million was the ideal place to conceal oneself. I camouflaged myself in a shelter that provided homeless youth with emergency housing for up to twenty-one days. After my initial orientation of schedule, procedures, chores, meal times, and counseling programs, each runaway signed on the dotted line. The fine print of my intake documents stated some hubbub about respecting the belongings and physical body of other residents and, technically, I didn't touch another homeless youth. 'Twas the night before Friday, just before midnight, not a teenager was moving, not even the mice. When out in the hallway, there started a clatter, all sprang from their bunk beds to see what was the matter. They witnessed me fraternizing with the opposite gender; I was found on top of the on-duty staff member. Our consorting, or me saving Doug's life, may have gone unnoticed if Doug's wheelchair didn't make such a commotion as we came crashing down, when I powerfully sucked the bone cancer that crippled his legs through his lungs. I tried to put myself in their shoes, the shoes that kicked my ass all the way out the shelter doors, and imagined what it must have looked like to them: like I was manically attacking a disabled man. Their eyes deceived them and I had no defense. Like when an able body person parks in the handicap space to lazily walk a shorter distance to their destination, and they can't wholeheartedly fight the ticket or tow expenses. Vindication would only come when Doug came to and retired his wheels. I only lasted about five days in the shelter, and the sixth day in the hospital until my legs worked again. Strike two.

The gym was a poor man's Ritz-Carlton, and thanks to my mother's concern of my back fat, I realized I'd never be homeless. All hail Planet Fitness! If any displaced, down on their luck individual could maintain a membership, they had twenty-four-hour shelter, cable, toilets, private showers, storage, massage chairs, and occasional free food. The judgement free zone even had a welcoming staff to clean up behind me. I enjoyed the all-inclusive facility for as long as I could during the day or for as long as no one got suspicious that I never actually worked out.

"Excuse me?" A skunk faced women pulled back the cheap vinyl shower curtains.

"What the fuck?" I swung my boobs around to face the unashamed peeping-tom boy girl. She crossed her arms in dissatisfaction.

"Well, you're not exactly my type either, Miss Mustache." The private shower stalls weren't so private. Since when did folks get so crudely bold with their sexual orientation? I supported the lesbians, but I also needed them to support my personal space; the only thing I was gonna share with this lady was my razor.

"It's come to our attention that not only have you offended management, but it is also believed that you're using the gym as your personal residence. You're no longer welcome here."

"I pay a lot of money to freeload…I mean work out here during the day, and the only person I've ever even spoken to was some ass-gina lady who stunk up the bathrooms." It hit me then. But to my defense, how was I supposed to know the lady who smelled like a bag of funky ass and vagina was a manager? I had to be careful who I offered a bar of soap and brillo pad to next time.

"Considering that your breath smells a lot like that managerial ass-gina that assaulted my nostrils that day, I'm convinced the two of you have conspired against me.",I added to my wrath, to which she called security and had my wet, half naked butt removed from the premises. I was being forcefully removed from my home. In an attempt to save face, I knocked over a pile of towels on my way out. Strike three. Being banned from the local library, shelter, and gym should have motivated me to drift to a new city— oppositely, it made me a glutton for punishment. A few more days in Mississippi couldn't hurt.

Hungry and eager to put myself in yet another unpleasant and embarrassing situation, I walked into the nearest fruit buffet. With nourishment on my mind, and little money in my pockets, I tossed a few dollars to the cashier and naturally began to serve myself from the smorgasbord of food. I'm sure stuffing the bananas, strawberries, and apples into my bag and not on a plate made me stick out like a sore, sticky finger thumb. My suspicious actions didn't go unnoticed, and I was soon approached.

"Excuse me ma'am, please come with me." Security escorted me to a private room to eat in peace—but there was nothing peaceful about it. They took my bag, and treated me like a criminal.

"Look sir, I paid for the buffet like everyone else— with the last of my money, may I add, and now you're harassing me. Why?" I was appalled.

"Ma'am, the Piggly Wiggly is not a buffet; it's a super-market. And you didn't pay anything for the items you took—you threw a hand full of used tissues at the store's stock boy before you put a bunch of fruit from the produce section into your bag," he enlightened me on the realities.

"That's preposterous," I defended my actions. The security guard refused to vocalize the discrepancies in my defense. He casually stared at me before playing back what the cameras had captured, assured that it would jog my memory. The footage was incriminating.

"Two things for sure: I believe that you believe that you're actually at a world-renown buffet in a Las Vegas casino, and second, I can find not one single fuck to give about this whole situation. I'm tired and have a headache the size of Serena Williams' ass, so I guess we both have shit for brains today." Every Monday, most people wake up with a deep disgust for their job, but his body language showed lethargic signs of illness and not so much the typical loathing signs of "I hate this fucking place and wish I was still in bed blues." He was truly in pain.

"I'm just glad you didn't try to run. The only thing I can catch these days is a damn cold. My whole body is weak." The seemingly in decent shape, thirty-something man had bigger problems than my petty theft.

"What's wrong with you?" I hoped he didn't mind me asking.

"Doc says there's a small tumor in my brain, Sallie Mae diligently believes I've actually put my lucrative bachelor's degree in finance to good use, my car broke up with me last night, and my pregnant girlfriend stopped giving me head because it's bad for the baby. There's a mound of pitbull's shit wrong with me, and now I'm contemplating if I'll lose my job if I let a woman, who is clearly off her meds, go with a friendly warning." His topflight name badge read Angelo Young. I felt sorry for him. His world was a category five disaster. The moment the universe informs you that your life ain't that bad is when you encounter someone whose life is, in fact, truly in the shitter. With a plunger in hand, I saw an opportunity for myself.

"If you let me go with a lovely fruit basket as a parting gift, I'll do what Sallie Mae, your girlfriend, and your doctor can't do." I made an intriguing proposition, and his eyes widened with anticipation of me buying my way out of this mess with sexual favors. Once he began to think with his other head, he was cured. I used my powers to take the world off of his shoulders.

"Never speak of me, or your cancer will return with vengeance." This time I left an unsettling and distinctive calling card behind. It was an empty threat, but my body count was getting too high not to implement some type of damage control. I feared the notoriety of challengers, and I hoped those I healed feared the return of the illness that challenged their existence. Confident that I covered my tracks, I enjoyed a delicious ripe apple on the way to the hospital.

# edible arrangements

The purpose of a vision board is to help clarify and maintain concentration on a specific life goal: a representation of what you want or need to manifest. It worked for so many people, so I gave it a try. I identified my vision, reinforced it with daily affirmations, and implemented action. I tore off the cleanest side of the box I'd slept on and marked WILL WORK FOR FOOD in big bold letters on it. I wrote my vision and made it plain. I believed that someone would take pity on me, and I stood on a busy intersection daily. My hard work and determination often only afforded me a strawberry milkshake and a side of bacon at Denny's, but the time off the streets with my feet kicked up was a prostitute's dream—not that I was a prostitute, but

I identified with their struggle, without the selling my ass part.

"Do you know how to thoroughly wash your ass?" A woman yelled from her car window.

"Excuse me?"

"A glass, do you know how to thoroughly wash a glass, a cup? Dishes. Do you know how to correctly wash dishes? I'm looking for a dishwasher. Your sign says you're looking for work." She offered me a job and not the offensive inquiry I'd first heard. Either I was overdue for the removal of earwax buildup, or my delusional interpretation contradicted reality. I experienced several misbeliefs when food was scarce. I was the paying patron at an exclusive fruit buffet one day, a cute little furry bunny bouncing on cotton candy clouds the next. And on this day, I was a dirty ass bum being offered soap—okay, so maybe the latter wasn't so far fetched.

"Yes, I am looking for work. What does it pay?" I asked the question, but it didn't really matter at that point. It had been weeks since my last episode, so I wasn't sure when I'd end up in a hospital bed with endless cups of Jell-O next. I would take whatever compensation she was offering.

"I'll need you for about five hours a day, six days a week. And in return, you can stay in the office above my cafe, and I'll give you a weekly stipend of twenty dollars, and all the cookies you can eat. I wish I could offer you more than that, but seems we're both in desperate circumstances." I couldn't beat that. I jumped in her car immediately. Kim Davis was a middle-aged woman who owned and operated a quaint tea shop that fashioned a varied assortment of freshly brewed, warm and cold teas, alongside light delicacies like bagels, scones, cookies, and cupcakes. The aroma that arrested my nose when I entered the street level storefront was succulently comfy, but I couldn't find ease in the tiny pastry heaven just yet. I was Gretel without a Hansel, lured inside with the promise of a soft bed, divine food, and a hot bath. My sweet hostess and new employer could have been a bloodthirsty old hag who was trying to cook and eat me. Or in modern interpretation, the sugary scent masked the human sex trafficking exploitation setup just beyond the mirage.

"This arrangement is unorthodox, and probably a cautionary idea, but I'll just pray you're not a murderer, because I need help. And you can pray the same of me, if it makes you feel better because you need my help. Besides, what's life without a little spontaneity!" Okay, maybe deceitfulness wasn't in her, and not much energy either; she seemed to have ran out of breath during the abbreviated tour of the six tabletops, delicious display case in the front end of the café, the aged, but functional back end kitchen, and my sofa bed surrounded by twenty years of documental buildup in the upstairs workplace.

"As you can probably tell, my strength is inadequate, and I can't tend to the café all by myself anymore, ergo the reason why you're here. Shower, and meet me down in the kitchen when you're ready my dear." Kim was weak, but generous, and indirectly told me I stank for the second time. She let me know the first time when she let down all four car windows to allow the brisk early morning breeze to transfer my days-old stench to the outdoors. One cannot be offended by the foul truth; I was grateful and just as adamant to shove a bar of soap in my mouth and push it out my ass. I showered and met Kim in the kitchen as directed.

I didn't believe the tantalizing fragrance of a freshly baked batch of sweet buttermilk buns could get any more captivating. No wonder Kim's visually tattered store stayed afloat in the midst of the surrounding Alabama contemporary rehabbed businesses. Kim had the recipe for success; she was literally the pied piper.

"Here's some chamomile mint herbal tea and scones before your first day of work. Let me know what you think." I thought the fluffy butterscotch scones and several cups of steaming liquid were amazing, and they gave me the itis. I wondered how my new employer would feel if I called in and went back upstairs for a nap. The ring of the bell on the front door snapped me out of my coma; it was time to earn my keep. I strapped on a plastic apron and gloves and got to work washing the pyramid of pots, pans, saucers, tea cups, and utensils. This was no simple household chore like I'd done many times before—this was a monstrous mess, deep dirty dive into a hot soapy sea of dishes. I was so drenched in water and sweat by the end of my shift that I could have skipped the earlier imperative shower I'd taken.

"I'll bring you my non-slip shoes tomorrow," Kim said with a laugh when I slipped and busted my ass for the fifth time. My amusement was hidden deep below my soggy sucker exterior.

"Does this job come with benefits?" My comedic delivery was the only dry thing on me; humor kept me from pulling her joker face down into the abyss as she helped me up.

"Believe you me, if I could bake up some health insurance, I would have done it a year ago when my back first started bothering me. Maybe I wouldn't have spent my entire life savings on medical bills, if I had insurance.

I've even dreamed of having the power to add magical therapeutic ingredients into my dough like Glinda The Good Witch—I'd heal the world for free, one cookie at a time." A small pinch of her believed in her adult fable. And so did I, and not just because I believed she had already manufactured and tested those so-called healing edibles, but because her sincerity made the bruises from my slips and falls inconsequential.

"Tell me about yourself. What's your story?" Kim and I sat in the back of the building where the sun got drowsy and eventually fell asleep. A single outdoor light lit our chairs and tray of brownies and milk. We shared particulars of our unalike existences, and somewhere amid my rosy, rewritten life story, devilish Disney voices interrupted me. My eyes that felt like overly-injected ass cheeks watched Kim's unmovable mouth and wondered how she spoke to my mind without making a sound; it was a great party trick. And everyone at the party were cartoon characters doing the Single Ladies dance. The pigs in the pin squealed at the jive turkeys who fed them turkey bacon; it was cruel.

"Call 911, somethings wrong with me." I was way passed totally spazzed—I was in a padded room, or needed to be in one. I couldn't tell the difference.

"Oh shit, look at you." Kim laughed and tortured me in my time of delusional despair. I was confused and panicked, until she took a break from being amused at my expense.

"I'm so sorry. I think I mixed up the batches of brownies." She admitted she drugged me, and then ran off like a remorseful dealer. Why had she forsaken me? Thank God she quickly returned with a pitcher of water. I tried to submerge my whole body in it like fucking Free Willy to wash my bad trip away.

"A couple of weed brownies won't kill you, but drowning yourself surely will. You gotta calm down girl—breath." Kim's reverse high-cology eventually sunk in. She made me believe I was coming down on a descending blanket of security, when in actuality, I just embraced the harmless accidental overdose. My superficial bruises and Kim's bad back disappeared as we danced to music-less music with animated farm animals. One of us was simply riding a familiar weed wave. I, myself, was on a splurge of enlightenment from both sides of my brain; logic and creativity penetrated my hemisphere and orgasmed. I truly believed that I miraculously understood life like never before. Undoubtedly, my intelligence was enormous and sure to eventually burst into a million specs of gold confetti. I was half-baked, and I didn't want it to end.

It ended, and the specifics were up for debate. I woke up on the kitchen floor, with foreign food trapped in my teeth, bra, and hair.

"Look who beat me to work this morning—and looks like you've already had breakfast!" Kim sang as she entered the back door and praised my punctuality. We laughed. I got up from the cold, hard surface and began my daily tasks. I may have looked like a wild stray, but I was on time for work for the first time, and I felt great—great enough to bypass essential grooming.

"I have to apologize again for drugging you, because that's the polite thing to do—but honestly, I don't feel bad. Last night was the most fun I've had in ages. It reminded me of my "fuck shit up" days, before me and my girlfriends surrendered to adulting. The good old days where bills, taxes, cellulite, and responsibilities didn't exist in our carefree hearts. It's a trap girl; growing up sucks old wrinkly balls!" She warned me. I wanted to laugh out loud, but I had yet to gargle away the demons raging in my mouth.

"Well, that's why I'm here—to help! I can help you with your adulting, and more around here if you need me to." Kim took me up on my offer just a few days later when she was too weak to flip the "we're open" sign that hung in the window bay. She needed a ride to her doctor's office. I would have said no considering all the sick people who make up a doctor's office, but she did only ask for a ride; I planned to lock myself in the car. Her pain encouraged my no-license-having ass to volunteer as her driver for the day. My unconfident posture in the driver's seat was evident; I gripped the steering wheel like loose dentures and sat so close that my boobs poked through the circular leather. I had only driven once before in my life—that one time I'd stolen that car from that mother and son freak duo. But at that moment, my driving skills derived from pure adrenalin. Kim couldn't drive and neither could I—it was a dangerous recipe for potential crash test dummies. I did the best I could to abide by the rules of the road, even if I didn't know what those regulations were. The muted radio allowed my ears to take exact directions from Kim's mouth, never veering off the short path to her appointment. While there was plenty of available parking closer to the building, the exteriors of every-one's cars would only remain undamaged if I parked far away. Kim's isolated Toyota was the only palm tree on a deserted island.

"Can you help me in?" Kim asked. My choices were to either bop Kim over the head and stuff her body in the trunk, or assist Gilligan off the island and into the building. I chose the rescue mission with the assurance that I couldn't catch a bad back from the other patients in the chiropractic office. And with my sole focus on being Kim's human cane, I never looked up to observe my surroundings or the big fucking cancer treatment center signs all over the place until we were inside. I felt betrayed, like Kim intentionally left out the fact that she had cancer. But then again, my new secretive friend didn't have one deceitful back bone in her cancerous body. She certainly downplayed her ailment; I was thinking she threw her damn back out in her younger years having wild sex or something. And why hadn't I sucked the cancer out of her already? By now my intuitive sense of being around someone with cancer should automatically sound off like gaydar. She helped me up off the floor several times, I should have gotten the sensation when we touched. I blamed the weed for clouding my spidey-senses. I stood frantically resistant at the door looking like a crackhead. I was a fiend in a dope house, a priest at a Boy Scout meeting; it was only a matter of time before someone's pheromones affected my civilized behavior. I tried to retreat and demanded to wait in the car.

"Don't be silly, come in and meet my friends," Kim yanked my arm. Her friends, what the hell did she mean her friends? It was either resist the urge or expose my side hustle to my new boss. But just like holding in a fart or eating only one chip was agonizingly problematic, this proved identically challenging. As soon as I entered the room and saw that her friends were sitting in a circle of recliners with IV lines pumping intravenous chemotherapy treatments into their veins, the timer began. It was only a matter of seconds before I pounced on one of them.

"Fight the urge, fight the urge Chance." My self-encouragement came from a book I skimmed through that boredom helped me find in Kim's office: 5 Techniques to Resist the Urge. That book was next to a how-to guide for reversing dangerous sugar cravings, seemingly the not-so-little Kim was getting high off her own supply. Not so oddly enough, I could identify with the impulses of a chronic overeater because taming any type of urge was the same across the board; knowledge, willpower, and patience were the foundations for resistance. Nervous deep breaths into my shirt that I pulled up over my nose, and my determination for keeping myself as close to the door as possible seemed to work. I'm sure my covered face and standoffish demeanor was offensive to a room of sick women, but I couldn't possibly survive an episode in a closed room; they would tie red bandanas around their heads and jump me to protect what they didn't understand.

"Hello ladies. Don't mind me, my breath just smells like a bowl of shit. It was a pleasure—I'll be in the car." I tried to make them feel comfortable, given my impolite behavior. The panicky sweat that wet my head, pits, and palms made the door handle slippery.

"Well, at least help me to my chair before you go." Kim was being real fucking needy; couldn't she see I was dying to get out? She leaned on me for stability, but I walked blindly. I kept my eyes closed and tried another technique: receptive visualization where I think of a movie in which I controlled the scenes. For some reason, my unhinged mind put me smack dab in the middle of a scene from Mission Impossible—how ironic. I slowly built the image of myself as Tom Cruise dangerously dangling horizontally in a sensitive room, trying not to set off any alarms. How the hell would I get out of the problematic situation undetected? I ran like hell—out of the room, down the hall, and straight to the car. It worked; well, something controlled my impending attack, I just didn't know what. My spastic strategies were all fine and dandy, but it was going to happen. It always happened, and now I could choose to have it happen close to home without an audience. Kim was an obvious choice. If cancer took her out, someone would eventually put me out of her house. I had to think of a plan, and fast.

On the drive back, Kim fixated on keeping her nausea submerged, and my mind knotted for a plausible approach to heal Kim without making things terrifyingly awkward. Then it came to me; I could play the man, between the man, to help the other man—like a phony liaison.

"What if I told you I knew someone who could help you?" I began to set up the deal.

"Help me how?" She spoke with her eyes closed and her head heavy on the headrest.

"Yeah, like someone to make you feel better." I was trying to stay away from any noun that referenced healing.

"Like a nice strong sexy man? That might make me feel better, sure." Kim's closed eyes envisioned the sexual healing she assumed I was speaking of.

"Eww, no. Like someone who can alleviate your disease altogether." I was vague, but eliminating her cancer was clear. She opened her eyes and turned her head to study the authenticity of my face and body language; did I express truth in my proposal?

"I'd try anything at this point, so bring on Magic Mike!" She gave me the okay for the mysterious arrangement; not that she truly believed me. She probably even thought I'd eaten more of those reality altering brownies.

I returned to the nonbeliever's house with her borrowed car and my doubled personality.

"Kim, we're here." I found her slumped over the side of her bed with her head in a bucket, which was perfect. Well it wasn't perfect that she was excruciatingly tossing her cookies, but it was accommodating that she was already in a dimmed room, laying down, and perhaps more receptive to a helping stranger in her personal space.

"Ok, my friend Magic Mike is here, but needs to keep his identity unknown so you'll have to wear this." I dangled a black sleep mask over her and begged for a boat load of trust—as much trust as a small piece of fabric over her eyes could provide. I walked back into the hallway and dressed for the part. Well actually my garb was for the part of a bootleg burglar and not so much a peaceful healer; limited resources were to blame; I had to work with what I had. I pulled my wild hair back, placed cotton panties over my face, the crotch covered my forehead, nose and mouth, leaving my eyes visible.

"Just relax; this will only take a minute. And you must promise to never speak of me or your cancer will return with vengeance." I attempted to disguise my voice with a deep baritone pitch while still sounding non rapist. I did the deed and rushed out of her house, but not before using her phone to call an ambulance to meet me a block away. The timing of suffering from spinal cancer just happened to fall on my day off. I was back to work Monday morning, feeling overly confident in my concealed structured crime.

The monotony of being an efficient dishwasher was only tolerable because of the music that blasted from my earphones. The hours passed by in my own little musical wonderland.

*"No, I don't want no scrub*
*A scrub is a guy that can't get no love from me*
*Hangin' out the passenger side*
*Of his best friend's ride*
*Trying to holla at me*


*I don't want no scrub*…oh shit!" I was startled by six pairs of eyes gazing at me, and then by a shattered plate. It was the first dish I'd broken since my first day on the job.

"Hello Chance, you remember my friends, right?" How could I forget Kim's sick lady gang. The organized group of women weren't criminals, ghosts, or goblins so they didn't scare me, but I had missed the memo about our late night kitchen mafia meeting; I was confused.

"I told them about what you did to me, and I was hoping you could heal them like you healed me." I was no longer undiscovered. I could understand sharing all your major secrets with your home girls, but Kim made a promise to never speak of her miracle.

"What? You been eating those brownies again. If your friends need their dishes washed, I can heal the tough dried stuck on food. No problem." I denied and played to my domestic strengths. What the hell happened to Kim's promise to remain discreet? Nurse Lisa wasn't joking about the HPV epidemic.

"You may have had panties covering your face, but it was definitely you. I recognized the smell of orange Ajax dish detergent and your dry wrinkly fingers." Clearly I was opposite of discreet.

"I'm not sure what you're talking about Kim." I hid my soapy prune like fingers behind my back.

"Please we need your help. We don't want to die." Their smiles turned to sad face emojis, the ones with the single tear. It tugged at my heartstrings. Not only could I relate to their suffering, I knew I could take them away. If they lined up, most progressed form of cancer at the front of the line, I could switch out those despaired expressions for any of the feel good ones in no time. They exalted me like I was Oprah—not the staggering positive and encouraging piece of her existence; they sought the superficial possibilities: the transfer of possessions.

"I'll take your cancer, I'll take your cancer, I'll take your cancer!" But I was no Oprah; I was no savior. They wanted the people's champ. What they got was a chump. I soothed their insistent appeals by nodding my head in agreement, when in my heart and mind I knew I'd excuse myself to the restroom, pack up my things, and sneak out.

# rock hard episode

Miami lies on the southeast side of the Florida Peninsula, and I lied on the furthest secluded corner on the beaches of Key Biscayne. The sands provided an incredibly comfortable sleeping surface. The sound of the waves was just the sedative I needed to relax; homelessness was challenging, but soon my luck would change. The calm tide brought what looked like a brown mini Snickers bar right up to me. The treasure could have been a dog's turd, or it could have been a sweet meal consisting of nougat, caramel, and peanuts all covered in milk chocolate. I scooped it up in my hand, washed off the grains of sand and prayed it wasn't a piece of shit left behind by an animal and their ill-mannered owner. I soon shared my peace and unknown uneaten treat with a major production crew clearing the area to assemble mounds of equipment. People tread back and forth between the white tents, and the main star eventually made their way onset. Being the true loyal fan that I was, I gave up the beach bum life and headed for the star's dressing tent. They were undeniably worth me exposing myself to a possible episode.

"I'm your biggest fan and I love you." My devotion and respect was unwavering since day one— a fulfilling connection that felt like it formed in the womb. I began to sing their praises.

"I got beans, greens, potatoes, tomatoes, lamb, rams, hogs, dogs, chicken, turkeys— you name it!" I didn't wait for permission;I grabbed breasts and legs. I had no shame, stuffing everything craft services laid out for the cast and crew into my mouth and bag simultaneously. A table full of free meats, breads, vegetables, chips, candy, fruit, cold water—I was food struck. The eagerness to be a groupie obstructed my windpipe and prevented air into my lungs. It was the first time I'd eaten in days, and I ruined it by trying to swallow everything whole.

"Whoa, chewing usually prevents choking." Someone pounded on my back until the partially chewed food landed right back on the table where I'd gotten it from.

I assumed it was security saving my life before throwing me in jail, and being locked up was potentially death for someone like me. I swung around and was met with a rock.

"No shit, Dwayne Motherfucking Johnson!" Literally and figuratively; I ran right into the naked pectoral of a World Wrestling Federation professional and sexiest actor on earth. It was the only other nipple I had ever touched besides my own. I wished he had body slammed me on the Krispy Kreme doughnuts and Applewood smoked bacon, satisfying one of my lusty food fantasies. But I guess saving my life was cool too. I thanked him with wide eyes and nervous giggles.

"Yeah, I love a good cheat meal, but you're badass when you die for the shit. Why don't you grab what you need and follow me." His genuinely distinguished voice invited me on his private yacht to pamper me. That's what I heard in my head, but in reality, we walked away from the water to his nearby trailer on the mainland. I wasn't sure if he wanted to trap me to wait for the authorities, or if he wanted me all to himself. I firmly maintained the latter, despite the rational argument that he was a happily married man with integrity and he wouldn't jeopardize that for a thieving girl who hadn't showered or shaved in I don't know how long.

I'm sure he could smell what my body was cooking from a mile away.

"So, tell me what's up? What's your name? Where are you from? How can I make today a better day for you? And yes, you can unequivocally use my private shower." He started in fast and furious and acknowledged my ass stank in the friendliest way possible.

"I'm Chance from New Orleans, I'm a big fan and currently homeless, and letting me use your shower is all I need to feel better, thank you."

"It's all yours, and stay as long as you like. I'll be on set. Everyone deserves a second chance right? Just don't steal my shit okay. Toodaloo motherfucker!" He laughed and left. He soon knocked and reentered the trailer, not even five minutes later, catching me with his toothbrush in my mouth. His gaze evoked interest; I knew he wanted me.

"Chance from New Orleans, right? Just curious, did you know a Malcom Johnson?" Dwayne asked. Of course I knew Obama Brown; how could I forget my first kiss and second victim. But how did The Rock know him, or know that I knew him? I shook my head yes without verbally incriminating myself.

"My nephew swore on his life that a girl named Chance sucked the life out of him. At first, I thought he was talking about his first blow job, and then I thought his first chemo treatment was frying his brain when he tried to describe how she cured him—healed his body, no trace of lung cancer to this very day. That was you, huh?" His eyes were filled with a twinkle of discovery and admiration. I didn't confirm nor deny, hoping my blank stare would make him feel stupid for even suggesting such accurate nonsense.

"Wow, it's true, isn't it? The universe works in amazing ways—small fucking world right? Cancer has taken out too many of us Johnsons, and I'm glad my nephew was spared. So, is it true? Did you cure him? Can you do the same for me, as a just in case?" I'd grant anything he commanded, if he rubbed me the right way. Some might say I was exploiting his misconception, or limited interpretation of my ability, knowing that I couldn't just turn it off and on, but those critics could only dream they'd ever encounter such a succulent, mouthwatering, and seductive construction of a man. So, fuck what they'd say. I gave the man what he desired.

"Sure, lay down." I was about to take full advantage of his preconceived notion that I could give him a get out of cancer free card. I straddled the waist of his 6'5 physique and leaned in exceptionally close, pressing my chest against his. He smelled like heavenly Under Armour.

"Just relax baby; close your eyes." I reassured him with gentle instructions in his ear. His face showed uncertainty, but he obeyed. With his divine upper lashes intertwined with the lower ones, I pleasured in the handsome structure of his face and bald head. I took my time, eventually pressing my lips against his. The tiny peppered hairs around his mouth pricked my skin, but I couldn't retreat; he owed me. I held him accountable for his nephew taking my lipginity and then calling the police. Dwayne truly did love his fans, because he just laid there and allowed me to relieve him of the cancer he knows he didn't have. I gave him a fabricated clean bill of health and he gave me eight seconds of uninterrupted juicy lips, and maybe even a little tongue. It was an even trade. We used each other. I hope it was good for him, 'cause it was damn sure good for me.

# jesus is my homeboy

The collected clusters of activated melanocytes increased the concentrated melanin cells of my complexion. All of that intricate mumbo jumbo just made the freckles on my face sound badass. The progression of my existence was chronicled in circular marks. I had given out so many second chances, I'd lost count. When I ran into other freckled faces, I often wondered if their repetitive badges of honor came from saving lives too, and if their beautifully spotted skin carried the sufferings of others, or if they were just naturally painted by their creator. Why couldn't my freckles be just that: freckles. My vacant stares went beyond the surface; I then fantasized about their warm beds, clean bathrooms, and jam-packed refrigerators. Feeling sorry for myself never seemed to get old. I got by over the years, but that good old saying "no good deed goes unpunished" rang true along with the aching groans of my empty stomach and the mounds of dirt that usually covered my funky body. The temporary stability I received while recovering in the hospital from an episode was the only thing I looked forward to. And if I desired staying in the hospital, that means I had to admit that I longed for the episodes that put me there. Shouldn't my charitable deeds manifest reliable food and shelter at the least? Or should I count my destitute blessings and refocus my selfish thoughts on the bigger picture—an understanding of my situation that included more than my rotting teeth and shitting in heavily wooded areas. I tried to keep myself encouraged daily, but contentment was few and far between. Not only had I aged by years, but the painful episodes were getting old as well. Especially since about the fifth episode in, an excruciating consequence was revealed.

Have you ever walked by a department store window and thought the mannequin moved, smelled rotten eggs and knew you weren't the one who dealt it, or worked late at night and felt like you weren't alone? Well, that was me. I'd been hiding in malls and underground sewers at night, trusting that the isolation would keep me from another suck fest of a terminal illness. Regrettably, there were flaws in my segregation. First of all, I was not immune to rodents. Coming face to face with a dirty grimy gutter rat forced me to stay above ground. Who knew Master Splinter was genetically predisposed to a high incidence of malignant tumors. It was disgusting, but if it weren't for me, the Ninja Turtles would have lost their sensei and adoptive father. Second, if I denied or prolonged the opportunity of the cancerous transferal for too long, the darkened coloration on my face would agonizingly pulsate. It was an intense feeling triggered in each freckle. Envision someone digging their sharp fingernails at the edge of a scab, getting a secure grip and ripping it from your skin with all of their might. The surface of my face felt like the equivalent of one big open and exposed sore covered in salt. Most people have a choice of how they wanted to give back to the people of their community; well my decision to donate myself to someone physically less fortunate was not an option. I was obligated to operate this one man non-profit charity no matter how much it hurt me. I was damned if I did and damned if I didn't. How could I rid myself of this demon disguised as a so-called gift? My journey for clarification continued.

Since way before inadvertently emancipating myself, our family had become religious backsliders as a result of poor attendance and irresistible comfort within the ways of the world. Apparently, God only showed up on Easter, Christmas Eve, and Mother's Day because those are the three days we got casket ready and dusted off our bible apps. And although it wasn't time for one of those said fashion events, my suicidal soul hoped the church I had just wondered into embraced more than just big fancy hats and patent leather shoes. Not only was I misplaced in the world, but more depressingly, I was lost internally. I had searched every known credible page with no evidence concerning my new affliction—every page except the pages of the bible. I never gave the collection of sacred scriptures any thought beyond just a simple accessory to my mother's outfit. But more recently, everyone was sporting God Is Dope apparel and hopefully he spoke of his dope divine healings in his autobiography. I anticipated verses of miraculous physical curing or anything of relation to provide comfort and reaffirm my sanity. I needed the pastor to give me the CliffsNotes to his copy, or at least a prayer and a Prozac.

I entered the sanctuary geared in my Sunday best— well the best that I could find at a lovely little boutique called the gym's lost and found box. Since the luxury of a washer and dryer was lost on me, the sweaty abandoned clothes were shamefully cleaner than all the recycled garb in my duffle bag. On a scale of musty and mustier, let's just say I desired more than just my sins to be washed away. Unable to keep up with the Christian Joneses, I casually crossed the holy threshold in a "Jesus Is My Homeboy" cotton T-shirt; I thought it was more appropriate than the "Squats Before Thots" tank top I had also found. An ounce of faith was the only accessory that kept me from being stylishly naked in the house of the Lord. An usher, whose name tag read Sister Rita, greeted me and graciously sat me in the back of the church, about five rows behind everyone else. Her smile greeted me, but her eyes condemned and found fault in my appearance and possibly odor. I guess the "Come As You Are" sign in the lobby was just for aesthetic decor. Once the praise and worship began, I played musical chairs and moved closer to the people. I joined in; my lips, hands, and feet praised as if I were in the choir.

"Stop it." A lady nudged my arm and spoke grudgingly. Apparently she wasn't impressed with my choice of praise. Since when was the Nae Nae and Stanky Legg banned from church? I wasn't trying to be disrespectful;

the hip-hop spirit made me do it. The choir and I eventually calmed and allowed the pastor to preach. He started in slow, and I found myself being more rapt in my eclectic surroundings than I was in his teachings; like the men who studied the big booty that stood up to give reverence, and the snoring deacon getting the best sleep of his life. But as he reached the meat of his sermon, the loudness in his delivery reemployed all of our attention.

"You are a sinner, contaminated with evil!" Why was he screaming at me? And why did his condemning message speak to me as if I were the only heathen in the sanctuary? I shamefacedly looked around to see if everyone knew he was talking about me too. I needed a church fan to cool off the conviction rising from my body.

"Your flesh is weak to the temptations of this world. Cast out those demons of fornication!" I quickly realized he wasn't condemning me; my flower had yet to be picked, but the lady next to me had clearly been plucked before.

"Oh Jesus." Her tone was hot and bothered, clutching her pearls at the sight of a man who had just left the altar. He was coming down the aisle returning to his seat, but you would have thought Jason Momoa was coming to splash holy water on her; she was so absorbed in lust under his sleek tailored suit and suspenders. His ferocious, peppered mustache eventually came into view.

"Oh Jesus!" My tone was disbelief. I quickly slouched down in the pew and used a nearby hymn textbook to shield my face. The bald head and hairy handlebar above his lips was hard to forget; I had never fought so hard during an episode as I did with him. The black eye he gave me wasn't a common symptom of the prostate cancer he also gave me. We were Ali and Frazier and then Tyson, his wife, jumped in the ring with a wooden bat and knocked my ass out. I wasn't ready to go round two with Colonel Sanders and his ride or die old lady.

"Sit up." A second nudge from the lady next to me would soon be reciprocated; she had one more time before I snatched her distasteful Easter Sunday hat and tangled wig and tossed it across the room. I sat up. He didn't see me, but two tiny prying eyes offensively gawked at me. I tried to ignore her, but she was staring me dead in my face; she refused to find some business of her own. She intrusively raised her germy miniature fingers in the air and began to connect the dots on my face.

"Point at your storm and tell it to move!" the pastor instructed the congregation. I mockingly pointed out the boogers that crusted her little nose and then aggressively signaled her to turn around. She was relentless.

"Turn around, snotty snoopy," I leaned forward and whispered. I didn't want our quiet war to get ugly, but she was pushing me to pull the Easter-Bunny-and-Santa-Claus-ain't-real card. Her ponytails retreated and slouched down in her pew. She found curiosity rummaging through her mother's purse, and I found concentration back on the pastor.

"We all have scars, above and beneath. They are a testimony, a testimony that you're stronger than you think. A resilient warrior and a peculiar treasure you are. Being the only one like you is a powerful thing." Wow, now he was talking to the uncertainty deep inside of me.

"Each of you are special and possess a gift that's meant to be shared with the world. Your gift only truly means something when you understand why you're supposed to share it. Because in this journey we call life, it is not just for you, it was given to you. In turn, bless those around you. It's a selfless gift. Share it." Damn, this guy was the DJ Khaled of churches. I felt all motivated and shit. There it was - not just the enlightenment I'd sought after, but there were those peering eyes again ascending up from the wooden pew, only now she had what looked like full blown chickenpox. She raised her fingers again to link my freckles. It became clear that she wasn't trying to share her highly contagious infectious rash with me. She used her mother's red MAC lipstick to impersonate me, to be like me; I was flattered. Her admiring smile brightened the room and along with guidance from the pastor, she defined my purpose. Although she didn't know the story behind my freckles, they were beautiful and meaningful to her and to those I could potentially help.

I received the encouragement and confirmation I needed, so it was time to go. My formulation of an exit plan was also fueled by the approaching collection plate. I couldn't afford my revelation. My broke feet darted for the sanctuary doors.

"I can baptize you and wash you of your sins today. I can see your reckless life of greed, pride, and wrath are all weighing you down. God wants me to tell you that you can be forgiven and washed cleaned." It was Sister Rude Rita again, projecting her personal deadly sins upon me. I recognized her kind: the resident holier-than-thou saint with a mission to save souls, or simply increase her number of baptisms. Her gratification for doing God's work was clouded by her craving to convict for attention and the praise of others. I may not have been to church in awhile, but discernment for bullshit was in me always. There were many Ritas walking among us. Sure, I could let her drown me in the baptismal pool where I'd reach up out the water and snatch off her synthetic wig, or I could share with her what God told me about living in glass houses.

"God wants me to tell you that you're a Christian twat and that your narcissism could use some watering down. How about we both jump in the baptismal pool?" A higher power moved me to knock Ridicule Rita down off her high horse and throw stones at the glass she, and many other Christians, liked to encase themselves in. The petty gods made me do it. Our eyes intensely locked for a moment while Rita contemplated acting a fool in her work place.

"I see you're not ready. Have a blessed day." Rita excused herself to exploit another soul. I left with new found encouragement.

It's been said that the man who has not even a suspicion of cancer in his body is granted extended carefree days, and the man who knows he's going to die, dies. Not to say that knowing is an automatic death sentence, but it's a difference of informed hope and informed hopelessness. It's mental; as a man thinketh, he is. But someone who knows more people who have died from the disease than they have fingers and toes is hard to convince that the transformation of their thoughts could therefore transform their circumstances. That's easier said than done. So, for all of us who can't grasp the beauty in the bullshit, maybe it is better when we don't know, and that's why I didn't enlighten my victims as to why I was about to attack them. I pledged to help those who didn't know—those who couldn't comprehend the growth of cells that invade healthy internal tissues and spread like roots of a tree. It's the innocence of a child that grants them blissful ignorance; they know their body hurts, but they're oblivious as to the future outcome of that pain. They're free, not yet tainted by experience—free to enjoy games, mud, cartoons, cake, burps, as no adult could. I was going to preserve as many bubblegum, adolescent snotty noses as I possibly could.

Directing my healing power towards the youth proved to be very predatory. Trolling recess playgrounds and neighborhood school bus stops made me a known predator. Inappropriately, I couldn't just choose a sick kid by looking at them—I had to touch them, the infectious fibers of their skin. Of course, it sounded a lot worse than the true intent. It was a feeling of tipping at the highest point of a steep roller coaster and dropping to my death that I searched for. The simple graze on their hand or arm was as pure as their untainted hearts, but to a parent, I was just a perv. Inquisitive adults began to side eye me; I couldn't hideout in the bushes peacefully. I needed to find a new way to prey on potentially ill children. A child may have no preconceived notions, but not a single judge would appreciate my benevolent predatory plea, and I was too cute for jail. I retreated from a park one Saturday afternoon when right in the middle of a game of tag I was asked, *"which one is yours?"* Ignoring the question only raised more for the concerned mother. She used her phone to take my picture, while I gathered my duffle bag and went about my business towards the nearest exit. My hurried feet met a four way stop where I waited for a black van to break and proceed; only it didn't. The dark executive Mercedes Benz looked familiar, only unlike the one I encountered in the hospital parking lot back home, this one's tinted window descended.

"Das ist sie." The driver stared at me as he spoke, but he wasn't talking to me. His words, whatever they were, prompted the movement of the side sliding van door. A broad-shouldered man lunged out towards me.

"Police." The driver saw a woman pointing an officer in our direction through his mirror and warned his partner in crime. He released his grip from my hoodie which made me plummet to the hard concrete. They took off before the van door could even slide shut. Little did they know, the cop was after me, and I could have probably used a ride—minus the kidnapping part. I took off too, on foot.

# the matrix

"So, what are you in for?" Their vocal chords were clearly compromised by religiously inhaled tobacco, but I couldn't put a face to the interrogator. When I opened my eyes, it was just as pitch black as when they were closed. Something was wrong.

"Am I in hell?" I questioned. I assumed I'd succumb to the last transfer of illness. Why else would I be hearing the dark villainous voice of Bane, smelling a mountain of cigarette butts, and perspiring like Whitney Houston's upper lip. But, on the other hand, how could my soul be condemned to a devilish afterlife? I mean, I was no saint, but I definitely had saint-like tendencies—mostly involuntary, but a healer still. Why wasn't

Beyoncé singing about my halo?! Why wasn't I in a heavenly paradise with Tupac, Prince, and Michael Jackson?!

"No, not exactly hell, but close…we're in the hospital." My mental rant was interrupted by who I thought was my new underworld cellmate. Confirmation that I was still in the land of the living soothed my anxiety.

"I'm Barb, two time survivor, and I'm in for the removal of my tits—I'm convinced cancer is an ass man. How about you, what part of your body is under attack?" Waking up in the hospital had become the norm, but realizing that Bane actually had breasts surprised me. If all of my senses were functional, my eyes and ears would have presumed Barb's birth name was Bob. My innate judgement made me an ass too.

"Well if my chart was in braille, and I could actually read embossed paper, it would probably mention something about a brain tumor. You can call me Chance." My speculation came from a combination of being in the cancer ward with bitter Barb, and my limited research of the child I had been shadowing. We'd both have to wait for the doctor to confirm my prognosis—not that I needed their professional second opinion.

"Damn mother, you smell like an ashtray." A third voice permeated our introductions. His tone was just as strong as the smoke-infused perfume his mother bathed in. And I had to agree, the inhalation was hard-hitting. Without sight, my detection of vibration was heightened. His loathing frustration trickled all the way down to the square-toe dress shoes that supported his impatient stride.

"Hey Chance, meet another man that wants to take something from me; as if permanently stretching my vagina wasn't enough." Listening to an alternative dysfunctional family in action was a sedative for the agony I was physically experiencing. They personified every corrupt family motivated by greed.

"If you'd just sign these documents, I'd let you and your vagina die peacefully." He expressed an ounce of empathy—his heart grew three sizes that day. My spidey senses told me he was both one in the same: financially and morally bankrupt, thus readily waiting to wave Barb's death certificate around in the air like a winning lottery ticket. Sadly, he was unashamed.

"Don't worry son, I will shower you with money one day. I'll make it rain right over your fucking grave, you little parasite!" Barb was determined to outlive her son, turn the cemetery into a strip club, and throw wads of cash into the air in his honor just to spite him. Their death match transformed into passive background noise as my concentration became the terminal pain that plagued my body. Morphine was on my mind; where was Nurse Lisa when I needed her?

"Good afternoon, ma'am. I'm Dr. Yumi, a pediatric surgeon here at the hospital. I won't be performing your emergency surgery tomorrow, but when I saw your case on the board, I was intrigued. I was studying to perform a similar procedure in the near future on a little girl named Semone. Only today, Semone woke up just as every child should, perfect and with perfect vision." His scent arrested my nose before his distinctive voice. It was a hint of traditional pepper, combined with a subtle blend of vanilla; it was deliciously yummy. But at that moment, the doctor could have smelled like a bag of farts and it would have been better than the cancer stick lying in the matchbook bed next to me. Without proof, the doctor waited for me to confess, assuming I was sweet baby Jesus healing the sick, reincarnated as a respectable misfit.

"Hello Dr. Yummy, that sounds like great news for… Semone was it?" I avoided his assumption, but I knew precisely what and who he was speaking of. What was the obvious, and who was a sweet little princess named Semone Owens. I was assigned to her room through the volunteer program for the sick children on the fourth floor of the hospital. I spent time singing with her, reading to her, and holding her tiny, little hands. Retinoblastoma was a cancer of the retina, commonly hereditary, that when left undetected and untreated, sadly resulted in a scheduled surgical procedure to remove her eye before the affected tissues spread to her brain. I hid out in the custodial closet and returned overnight to restore what was rightfully hers: vibrant colorful youth.

"You see, retinoblastoma generally appears in very young children, so I can't understand how you're at this stage at your age. When did an ophthalmologist detect your disease?" His British inflection was not only fascinating, but absorbing; my ears studied his tongue in search of the unpronounced consonants. I wondered if his looks matched with what my other senses approved of. However, my eye cancer trumped eye candy, so I dismissed him without prejudice.

"I hate to cut this unexpected blind date short, but you're just not my type, or even my doctor. I'd like to be alone now, thank you." My circumstances didn't allow for tender interactions, I swiped left. I'm sure he'd be back, but I'd be healed and gone by then.

Just as the many times before, my body was restored, and it was time to sneak out like a bandit in the night. Staying until the morning would definitely invite all the pesky questions like "what is your name and the name of your insurance provider?" Often times, I felt corrupt for skipping out on the bill, but the minimal drugs, unsavory food, and rent for one night's stay was incomparable to saving a life. According to my estimation, my bill would be forever paid in full. My 20/20 eyes navigated through the dark as I grabbed my few belongings and headed for the door.

"Well, ain't that a glitch in the damn Matrix." Agent Barb caught me.

"The blue pill ends the story, and the red pill keeps you in fairyland. Which one did you take, and do you got any more?" Her jokes led me to believe she may have habitually indulged in more than just tobacco. Barb reminded me of the addicts I often passed on the streets, chasing that next high no matter what it was.

"I took both, and the Viagra I found under my bed." I teasingly overindulged as well and joined my soon to be ex-roommate on her bed. Our legs dangled off the side.

"Okay so what gives? Are you in here smoking on the low? Why do you smell like a damn house fire?" I had to know. Barb reached to the left side of her body and repositioned the Mary Poppins bag that crossed her body onto her lap. It clung to her like an oversized designer colostomy bag. She then invited me to peek inside, to which all I witnessed was mounds of ashes.

Barb dug deep inside and pulled out secondhand trea-sure. Stacks and stacks of cash shaken free of debris and positioned in my hands. She cleverly hid what money she could from her son. I refused it.

"Take it, I don't need it where I'm going, and neither does my evil son. I heard that child doctor who was in here yesterday; you saved that little girl, didn't you? Well if you're an angel, consider this my down payment for a spot up there in the sky." She wanted me to secure her a place with the landlord.

"What if I told you there's a chance I can come back for you?"

"Don't waste any of your nine lives on me honey—cancer is only a result of my decisions; I did this to myself, and I can live with that…or not." She laughed at her own morbid humor. She was at peace, and I respected that. I put the money in my bag and we said our goodbyes.

A sum of income and disbursement for a defined period of time is described as budgeting. Logically, I should have allocated Barb's generosity for the specific purpose of sustenance and shelter, stretched over many months. Immaturely, being financially respon-sible was in the eye of the beholder, and adulting just wasn't in my financial plan. I blew through eighty-five percent of ten thousand dollars in three weeks. I spent it fast, recklessly, and without care. I kicked my feet up in a modest room at a Ritz Carlton for about three hundred a night (at an inflated rate of course, because I had no credit card for incidentals). I met a girl who worked in reservations when we were both shopping for hoodies at Bloomingdales. She hooked me up with an employee discounted room, and I hooked her up with a hefty commission for doing so. And why not, I had it to give. I even tipped the valet guys, and I didn't even have a fucking car. I was careless, but carefree for once in a long time. When my funds came to an end like a fair-weather friend, my freckles decided to start pulsating: a painful sense of reminder that I wasn't rich and had more significant shit to do than pop expensive water bottles. I was like a vampire who needed to feed—a vampire who deliberately rubbed poison ivy all over their face like night cream. The rash of excruciating swelling and itching forced me to check out of plush paradise and head back to reality.

I reverted to the room where I bunked with Barb. One could say I returned to help Barb hide more money from her son, but I told myself that I was going to return to save the life she'd given up on—then be rewarded with more of her money. Neither scenario occurred; Barb's son won their fight the day after I left the hospital last. But there was no time for a second of sorrow; another life had to be chosen to relieve my pained face. It was like curing a hangover with more alcohol; I cured one pain with more pain. It was a vicious cycle. I snuck in and out of the rooms on the fourth level of the hospital until I found her:nine year old Lizzy White had been diagnosed with breast cancer. I'd read once that young children and adolescents had just a one percent chance of developing breast cancer. Lizzy was rare, one in a million, a baby unicorn, and that's why I chose her. The new-age hospital's digital patient charts gave me easy access to her information, and she was scheduled for a total mastectomy to remove the harden lump from her chest. I knew I could take her place, granting the opportunity for the development of both her breasts to dress in pretty, lacy bras one day, but still my emotions surfaced as if I couldn't heal her. Great sympathy for women young and old fell heavy on me. At one point, Lizzy's biggest concern was not getting caught with pink eyeshadow on, and then all of a sudden her body was hijacked by disease, anguish, and fear. It was invasive. It was destructive. It was unfair. The salty teardrops that ran over my already throbbing freckles burned like hell.

"Fuck!" I manned up and got on with it, but as soon as I took her cancer, it attacked my left breast. An instant lump formed and my shirt dampened from the bloody discharge of my swollen inverted nipple. The massive pain sent me into shock. I flashed in and out of consciousness. I didn't make it far; good thing I was in a hospital.

"I've seen this patient before. Hello, do you know where you're at? What's your name ma'am?" Who I assumed to be a doctor ran a miniature flashlight over my pupils. In the next moment of awareness I felt myself being poked with needles and latex fingers inspecting every inch of my body. I preferred more meds and less genius doctors doing their jobs.

"I've never seen such an invasive case. I'd recommend a total mastectomy. I'm sure this has spread." They spoke over me as if I had no say so. I had to speak up for myself.

"All my life I had to fight, but I ain't never thought I'd have to fight over my own body! I loves doctors, God knows I do. But I'll kill em' dead fo' I let them take my titties." For some reason I channeled Sofia from The Color Purple in an effort to save my boobs. Clearly my personal declaration was medically induced, but hopefully conveyed my lack of consent for any surgical procedures. I'd made it years without falling into the hands of an over ambitious doctor who immediately cut first and assessed later; I needed the streak to continue. I could understand their position; it was like dangling a celebrity in front of a plastic surgeon—they'd take the bait. But if they could just fight the temptation for twenty-four hours, I'd walk away with both my breasts, shoulders, knees, and toes.

# lair, lair

The thick, underground cemented walls were specifically designed to prevent mine and the previous victim's screams from being carried to the external ears that could rescue us. The atmosphere was murky, but the sophisticated surgical instruments skillfully positioned on a sterile tray gleamed. The clamps, retractors, syringes, and scissors radiated just as my mother's polished jewelry. It was windowless and damp with a scent of death. The intended dread and intimidation of the torture chamber I was in was working. I was ready to confess every one of my secrets, and a few of Olivia's too. This snitch would gladly accept her stitches if it meant I'd be freed from imprisonment. The violent psychopath may not even have wanted to dig into my psyche to reveal my skeletons or innermost vulnerabil-ities at all; they may have just wanted to cannibalism and chill. The question wasn't what would I do, but what would Hannibal Lecter do to silence the Chance?

"Alright freak, what do you want? And you should know I have a belligerent display of vaginal herpes." I spoke to the back of a starched knee-length labora-tory coat.

"Me the freak…you sure about that?" I'd heard that foreign tongue before. My mind raced to put a face with the unique accent before he turned around. It was Dr. Yummy. Damn, he was scrumptious. The only good looking doctors I'd seen were on scripted tele-vision shows; all of my previous physicians were held together with Poligrip and Bengay. Too bad he was a psycho killer; we could have made a cute couple.

"I'm not the one sucking the life out of little chil-dren." Stefan Yumi didn't need to inflict pain or break out the kryptonite to expose my little secret. He already had a few pieces, but my sealed lips wouldn't help him complete the puzzle.

"So, what exactly are you?" His intelligence wouldn't allow him to guess what he couldn't scientifically explain.

"I'm currently exactly a prisoner." I spoke to his intel-ligence and stated the obvious.

"You're not being held captive. This morgue is the only place I could treat you without interrogation from doctors and authorities." Stefan revealed himself to be less of a creepy threat and more of a helpful ally. My hands weren't bound, I was respectfully clothed, and the room wasn't so dark and horrid. Maybe my eyes embellished my state of despair a bit.

"Treat me?" I needed further enlightenment as to how and why he designated himself as my offsite oncologist. Not that I wasn't skeptically grateful. Dr. Yummy went into great detail about the diverse cancerous tumors and growths he'd explored and in all of his years of clinical research with the National Cancer Institute. He had never experienced a single patient with two separate destructively diagnoses be completely healed of both. He spoke in geek, just as many of my doctors over the years did, but I was fascinated by his accented pronunciation, so I hung on his every word, especially the part where he described how he initiated an induced coma so I could bypass the suffering while I healed.

"I administered a controlled dose of pentobarbital. The sedation placed you in a temporary coma." He spoke like a seasoned professional, but looked about eighteen. Given I didn't exactly see him in our first encounter, I never questioned his age. If I had to guess, with his knowledge and experience, he was easily pushing fifty-five, but he wore it impeccably well due to the fountain of youth he drank every day and leeches that sucked the toxins from his blood every night.

"Although ethically erroneous, the fact that you survived the previous cancer, I was encouraged to move your body before the unnecessary removal of ductal carcinoma…your breast." Stefan reminded me to check for my boobs. I quickly groped myself. My B cups still sat on the shelf, thank God. Saving my tits granted him two minutes of uninterrupted appreciative dialogue, but then I was throwing up the deuces.

"So, what are you a black Doogie Howser or something?"

"I'm twenty-two, and I can assure you that I'm more than qualified in my field and beyond," Buzz Lightyear emphatically pleaded his case.

"Thank you for your help, boy genius, but I gotta go." I got off the cold table and grabbed my sneakers. His captivating brown eyes followed me from behind his Gucci frames.

"You could stay here, if you'd like, and I could help you." His strong jawline held a nerdy, flawless smile. This guy was going for some type of good looking Samaritan award.

"You're kind, but I'd rather not live in a human refrigerator for the dead." I was fronting; a cold dark apartment with dead people actually sounded like a come up. If the rent was less than a penny, I'd merrily roommate with the corpses.

"My grandfather left me this morgue, but he also gifted me the shack above it. I know it's odd to stay in a stranger's home, but something tells me you don't exactly have reliable shelter. And I have food." He lured me in like a fat kid; food was my kryptonite. Visions of a warm grilled cheese sandwich had me ready to negotiate the terms of my new living arrangement. A wealthy doctor picking me up off the streets and taking me home could have been promising; what would Julia Roberts do? I, of course, followed him.

My dirty Jordans observantly scuffed against the marble floors that stretched throughout the unparalleled so-called shack. The wide open space was enclosed with enormous floor to ceiling windows, positioned to take full benefit of the astonishing Savannah, Georgia views. Dramatic four inch baseboards and vaulted ceilings with crown molding complimented each room furnished with distinctive decor. A scattered gallery of priceless unconventional paintings garnished the walls, and the gourmet kitchen was a chef's dream, with stained granite countertops, stoned backsplash, custom black solid oak cabinets, professional stainless steel appliances, and a sub-zero side-by-side refrigerator; high-end was an understatement to describe the superior touches. It wasn't a home, it was a showroom. Now I'd become accustomed to moderate, luxury living, but it was rare to find a man with such exquisite taste who wasn't either gay or married to a woman who insisted on an exclusive interior designer.

"Quite the run down shack you have here. Ever thought of rehabbing?" I watered down my admiring comments. I may have been impressed, but I didn't intend to stroke his ego—or anything else for that matter. I sat on an ivory quilted counter stool with my duffle bag clinched to my chest. I waited for two things: Stefan's partner or wife to disapprove of his stray patient, and the castle's animated enchanted staff to sing and dance while they prepared my meal.

"Aww, you girlfriend?" A petite woman with broken English appeared in the kitchen. She looked all too happy to find fresh blood in the house.

"No, Mary, she's not my girlfriend. Even better, she's a superhero with super powers. Chance will hopefully be our new houseguest,, and in return we'll keep her identity a secret." Stefan introduced me to his friend and housekeeper.

"Not a houseguest. Just call me a freeloader; it's much more glamorous." They didn't laugh. I too agreed that my comedic delivery was traded with starvation. I refreshed my greeting.

"It's nice to meet you, Mary. Did Stefan lure you in with the promise of food too?" I wanted to redirect everyone's attention to my sunken belly, to which they did laugh.

"Maybe not a homie lover friend, but you must be special. Stefan never bring girl home." She grinned. Mary was funny.

Grilled cheese sandwiches accompanied our modest, leisurely exchange; Stefan pried, and I ate while nodding my head. I would have preferred a steak, but prolonged hunger made the simple recipe taste just as decadent.

"I'm not an alien or some freak of nature." I swallowed the remaining water, abandoned the empty glass, and rewarded Stefan's inquisitiveness.

"About twelve in the morning, the day of my seventeenth birthday, I found myself inhaling the life of my best friend from her body. The destruction of one's brain when they digest that they've taken a life is debilitating—more like bat shit crazy. Then imagine the implosion once you comprehend that they're still very much alive. You want to appreciate the vindication, but you're focused on the decomposition of your own body. Long story short, I involuntarily relieve people of cancer—no matter what stage they're at, or if they even know they have it. It progresses over a 24 hour period once it's inside my body, and then my body heals like Wolverine. I'm in permanent remission of each cancer once it passes; I've yet to repeat the same disease twice. But with so many types of cancer, there are so many battles yet to be fought. I get a solid five free days after each episode; however, I can't predict the next time I'll be plagued with death. I can fight the urge, but never for too long."

"How many people do you think you've saved?" Stefan asked.

"Well, it's hard to keep an accurate database, given my dying desire to be homeless, but I'd just have to count the spots on my face. These freckles only arrive after I've saved a life—two or three spots at a time." I could only guestimate.

"Like the soldier's medal—it's awarded to individuals for acts of heroism and bravery. The award is the highest honor a soldier can receive for saving a life." Stefan linked courageous servicemen who put their lives on the line to my tiny scars; the connection didn't seem like a worthy comparison.

"You do realize that you're the cure for cancer right? Stefan made me larger than life with a distinction too much for one girl to bear.

"You like superhero, with crappy costume. No offense." Mary gave her shady two cents.

"Yes, the cure part sounds all lovingly charitable, but what about the other part? The suffering and torture? Would you want what I have? The cure doesn't come without the curse. And not all superheros wear capes." A costume was the least of my worries; I was a nonconformist…but first and foremost, I was too broke for a spiffy get-up.

"Or soap." Mary was a comedian.

"If you stay here, you'll come to appreciate what you have. You can just focus on the good, and I'll take care of the other part." Stefan went on to explain just how he was beneficial to me and me to him. As an oncologist, he had access to the very cancer patients I needed to feed off of, and his skills as an anesthesiologist would put me in a deep sleep until the disease passed. He made it all sound so uncomplicated.

"Truth is, I need you more than you need me. I dread looking into the eyes of someone who's either going to die from the disease or the deadly chemicals we pump into their bodies and tell them they're going to be okay. Is there a such thing as lying faith? Well with you, I no longer have to lie." His confidence in me was bigger than his seven thousand square foot house we lounged in. He was very convincing.

"You'd have your own room, bathroom, and free reign of the house, which includes a fully stocked kitchen with your own personal chef." His sales pitch improved with each minute I stared at him without an answer. He tried to upsell me with upgrades and add-ons to close the deal—shit, he had me at grilled cheese sandwich. I stayed.

I couldn't sleep. I guess that's what happens when you're comatose for twenty-four hours. I had locked myself in my new room as if I were really somehow protecting myself; if Stefan and Mary wanted to grossly terrorize me in the night, no lock that they probably had the key to would stop them. But I did keep my clothes on and made sure not to dig in my nose in case they were watching. The only way to feel free from the unfamiliar was to familiarize myself with the lay of the land. Curiosity would either kill me or my insomnia; I didn't have shit else to do. I roamed the gorgeous floor plan. The original blueprints may have been vintage, but the rehab was epic. The present-day upgrades didn't match the exterior fronts of the beautiful homes outside the windows. I bypassed the areas I'd already visited earlier that day and found myself in the opposite end of the house where there was a gym, laundry room, and an impressive multilevel library. I sought for an enchanted rose with wilting petals, but there was no magical flower or books that triggered an opening to a secret room. I did find an open glowing door at the end of the hall that called for me. Inside, were carpeted stairs that whispered the bad boy voices of Will Smith and Martin Lawrence. Following each step led me to witness the most controversial, but inexcusable act taking place. Mary was sitting before an enormous theater screen in a stretched leather recliner using needles to manipulate yarn into a hideous garment, taking small breaks to bite across all four rows of a kit kat bar.

"What the hell are you doing?" I was appalled. What would drive a human to devour the chocolate as a whole? The ethical way was to snap the four bars apiece and eat them separately, savoring its crunchy sweetness. I knew these people were freaks.

"What do you plan to accomplish by doing that?" I was concerned.

"I'm making you a costume." Her intentions were far more fucked up than I thought. No ma'am, she was not creating an ugly pot holder for my face.

"Oh that's nice, but I'm claustrophobic." The thought of dull yellow and grey interlocked fibers against my skin made me itch with suffocation.

"I'm just pulling your tits girl, knitting relaxes me and keeps me from slappin' a bitch," she laughed. She was cool, and could be the perfect Alfred to my Bruce Wayne. A loyal, sarcastic, and tireless butler was a great accessory to my mysterious life. She reminded me of Olivia in ways—I wondered if Stefan would let me keep her.

# hostel environment

My new memory foam mattress seamlessly conformed to every inch of my body, relieving the pressures of the world. It provided more support than the defiled restless surfaces I had become accustomed to. The sensation of finally getting sufficient quality sleep was crucial for my mental and physical health. Peaceful caress curved quickly to violent panic.

"Who the hell is in my damn bed?!" I was jolted from serenity to find a very agitated bear coming for my golden locks. Stefan swiftly appeared to hold her back and forced her out of the room. I sat on the bed in shock, frozen with my ears to the commotion in the hallway. The uproar fell silent, and I took the noiseless intermission as an opportunity to release my defensive fists and gather my belongings. I cautiously dressed in my shoes and hoodie, grabbed my duffle bag, and stood calmly by the bed awaiting the precise moment to exit the madhouse. Although the fussing had stopped, I wasn't dumb enough to blindly step foot outside the room without making sure I wouldn't get clocked by Stefan's livid girlfriend waiting for me around the corner.

"It's my bed!" She cried.

"What are you doing here? Calm down!" He pleaded. My Yelp review of Hotel Yummy would certainly be unfavorable, with emphasis on the "Ho-tell". The chaos once again commenced, but thank God the turmoil in her voice fueled her feet away from my innocent blood. I heard heavy and hatefully thumps striding down the hall. Usually I witnessed such atrocious and pathetic altercations on reality TV. Yeah, I was aware what it may have looked like and most women would undoubtedly identify with her rage that boiled at a destructive altitude. It looked like her man brought home a random chick and sadly, she was convinced that I was intentionally there to ruin her life and relationship. She was determined to protect her territory and set the scene for an episode of Snapped. I didn't know about her just like she didn't know about me, but by no means was I a punk. I was just a charity case who preferred to keep all my hair and teeth where they belonged. Removing my pretty face from the boxing ring would allow this angry lady a chance to replace her misplaced anger. I was out. If I had to fight for a bed, I could have stayed on the streets. I showed my gratitude nonetheless.

"Thanks for your help." After rolling my eyes back into place, I gave Stefan the same evil stare the jilted mental patient gave to me as I headed for the door.

"No, leave me alone and go take care of your sugar mama." I pulled away from Stefan who tried to grab my hand and lure me back into the cougar's den. I had nothing against women who pursued sexual activity with significantly younger men—I just preferred not get clawed in the process.

"It's not what you think, I promise. Can you at least let us explain over breakfast?" Damnit, he just had to mention food. I was a prisoner to the smell of pork and pancakes streaming the air. Of course I stayed.

Early afternoon set the tone for our outdoor rooftop brunch. By my side sat Stefan, and across from us, the face of a remorseful woman about twenty-five to thirty years Stefan's senior. Instead of Stefan depositing his views and opinions of her into my mind, he thought it wise to allow me to formulate a proficient analysis of my own.

"I do apologize for my outburst. I forgot where my room was and when I…" She expressed regret, but strangely got lost in her thoughts. She looked to Stefan for help.

"This is Anita Yumi, my mother. She has what's called chemo brain. It's a term used by cancer survivors to describe one of the debilitating side effects from treatment. She experiences confusion, short attention span, and memory problems." Stefan defended his mother as her doctor and loving son. I felt sympathetic and a little silly. I wished I had come to a responsible and dignified conclusion before I tried to run out, but in all fairness, my sensibility was clouded by my face beating up Mrs. Yumi's hand.

"She doesn't live here anymore, but she's welcome whenever she pleases. Right Mom?" Stefan caught the eyes of his mother's mental fogginess, to which they shared a warming smile. I admired their bond and Stefan's moral principle to promote a healthy environment in every aspect of his life: the hospital, his home, and with his mother.

"No apologies needed. I understand. It's very nice to meet you Mrs. Yumi." I tried to engage her attention as her eyes followed soaring birds that danced over our heads.

"Well, it's not very nice to meet yet another groupie stray. My Stefan is an established man who truly has no time nor need for freak freeloaders like yourself, but unfortunately, he has a soft spot for the ho…" Her smiley face switched to an incurable look of constipated annoyance. And was she about to call me a hoe? Chemo brain my ass; I knew passive aggressive when I saw it. Anita had what's called an inappropriate relationship with her son. Cut the fucking cord already. Mary passed behind Anita with a tray of fresh fruit; her rolling eyes warned me that it was time to make my dramatic exit. I made sure to stuff my mouth and pockets with free food before I disrespectfully replied.

"She was going to say a soft spot for the homeless." Stefan clarified before our two outspoken personalities diplomatically clashed.

"I don't need translation, but clearly someone at this table needs to get a fucking clue or a big sign with big letters directing her to the door. You're not welcome here you…" Given her superior bitchy charm, I wish I could say what happened next didn't make me laugh, but the white liquid that released from one of the glorious birds above splattered on her bottom lip. I swapped my vengeance words and middle finger for tickled laughter. Divine intervention gave her exactly what she asked for—a big ass sign. It stopped her from talking shit, literally. Before the sight of her thick lip gloss could make everyone throw up in their mouths, the perpetrator turned victim and scurried her petty leather boots from the table; she was off with her head.

"I'm going to get her back to her home, but please don't go anywhere. I would like you to stay." Stefan left to return the queen to her throne.

"You must be birdie whisperer; I could never get her to shut up." Mary joined me and we raised the cold lemonades to our lips. I wondered if I could hire my feathered friends to go troll Sophie's lips. I extended my stay, but made sure to keep my room locked.

The narrative of my eccentric life wouldn't be complete with just a single cameo from a villain; Mrs. Yumi's antagonistic behavior was malicious, but delivered pure comedic occurrences. If we had crossed paths earlier in life, I would have been happy to relieve her of the disease that had shaped her random wickedness. Although, I think I preferred the entertainment that her bat-shit crazy "chemo brain" had to offer.

Her next attempt to run me off involved her beloved best friend, Denzel. She carried the Pomeranian fluff ball around in a large designer shoulder bag, where his beady eyes and tongue peered over the side and left a funky crust on the iconic Louis Vuitton monogram. Being the responsible mother she was, Mrs. Yumi added extra high fiber to Denzel's diet, opened the door, and let him out to do his business. Her parenting came into question when she also added laxatives, opened my bedroom door, and let him piss and shit everywhere while I was in the shower.

"What the fuck?" My fresh Dove toes stepped right in foul dookie. There was only one way a dog who obviously ingested a stool softener got into my room and closed the door behind himself—Anita Yumi. She had officially declared war. If there was an upside to poverty without a pot to piss in, it was that I developed an art skill for shit-handling. With the help of Mary, we rapidly drenched my floor with disinfectant, wrapped Denzel's leaky butt in a grocery store bag, and tossed the compact puppy down in the morgue. We both casually walked in the kitchen where Mrs. Yumi sipped her newly brewed cup of coffee.

"Hello Mrs. Yumi, how are you today?" I greeted her with joy. She seemed thrown by my reaction, or lack thereof.

"Denzel. Denzel honey, come to mommy. Denzel Washington Yumi, bring your ass here now." She casually called for her dog. Her demands quickly became frantic as she disappeared off in the direction of where she'd purposely left him: in my room. Mrs. Yumi returned after she found no trace of her little shit, or his shit.

"What's wrong?" I knew what was wrong, but I'd show my hand once she showed hers.

"Hush puppy!" Mary raised the bet when she loudly whispered into the kitchen's trash compactor before she closed it and started the electric waste compressor.

"What are you doing? Are you crazy? Denzel!" She ran over and tore open the small appliance.

"Hush Puppy, like the seafood restaurant—for dinner. Estas loca." Mary and I giggled as we watched a desperate woman who could dish it, but not take it. She called her real son, the pound, and the police to no avail. We let the dog out of the bag about an hour later.

Our third encounter happened about a week later when I opened my bedroom door one afternoon and found her sitting criss cross applesauce in the hallway. As if staging an Indian style sit-in wasn't odd enough for a fifty something year old lady, she was also protesting my presence while being butt fucking naked. I smirked and closed my door. She might have thought that her voyeurism would make me uncomfortable enough to leave, but instead, I joined her naked reindeer games. Just minutes later, I reopened my door and walked out with my boobs and cheeks freely hanging too. Surprisingly, this offended Mrs. Yumi...especially when I began doing deep lunges and squats right in front of her.

"You're disgusting." She angrily mumbled under her breath as she got her bitter behind up and retreated. Mary simultaneously came down the hall with a Swiffer WetJet without judgement or investigation of us bare naked ladies, but she did stop to give me dap. That was two for me and zero for Stefan's mother. She tried desperately to get on the scoreboard during round three. My villainess roommate, who wasn't truly a roommate, but a welcomed nutty intruder, greeted me at the front door.

"What's up Mrs. Yumi, how are you?"

"Never mind that. I'm going to give you twenty minutes to pack your bags and get out. You're no longer welcome here." She was confident in her demand.

"I have respect for you. I really do. But I don't have time to play today—my stomach hurts. Can you come back tomorrow?" I wanted to reschedule our playdate so I could go alleviate my bubble guts.

"Okay. I'll just call the police and let them help you vacate the premises." Her intimidation tactics might have scared me if she could even make good on her threat. Her two front teeth objected her false claims to the dispatcher; her fabricated dental flipper flipped right out.

"Hey Mom, what are you doing here?" Stefan opened the front door and saw his mother scramble to stick her teeth back in her mouth to answer the question.

"Oh, Mrs. Yumi is just serving me with a not-so-verbal eviction notice." I answered for her.

"Mom, I love you, but you're not the landlord because this is not your house. Therefore, you cannot terminate the tenancy of my houseguests." He took the toothless pitbull inside, and I followed in behind them. I felt it was time to break the lease of our friendly rivalry. I needed to set things straight and put this woman in her place; I refused to let her fuck up a good thing for me. Stefan took a call, and I took the unsupervised moment to initiate a civil and logical discussion between us ladies.

"Can we chat?" I tried to be diplomatic, but Mrs. Yumi rendered an incurable look of annoyance as if she was sickened by my mere existence.

"This little game we've been playing is fun and all, but I would really like to establish and maintain a positive friendship with you." I truly meant my words; I had no real beef with her.

"I understand that my son is a man, and you're simply here to cater to that, but what I can't understand is why his whore is talking to me. You're trash." Mrs. Yumi drew her line in the quicksand, and before I knew, I had crossed it and sank. Being unfairly insulted triggered a rage in me; I had her in a choke hold on the floor. Banging her head against the marble was truly uncharacteristic, and engaging in violence was extremely contradictory of my usual heroism. I'd gone rogue. My unconscious retaliation was justified, but when my disrespected imagination was done running wild, I snapped out of my violent daydream and continued in reality.

"Can we chat?" I tried the diplomatic approach again.

"I respect you, and I respect the expectations you have for your son, but I think you've misunderstood our dynamic. I'm here for business only." I spoke to her refined intelligence.

"Getting paid to spread your legs doesn't make you a business woman." Damn, she was a tough nut to crack—pun intended. I would never win with this lady, so instead of viciously wrapping my hands around her wrinkled neck, I simply spoke to her refined crazy side.

"Stefan is great, but he's not exactly my type, if you know what I mean." I sent an air kiss across the room over to Mary who had no clue what we were talking about. She picked up what I was putting down, and she sent one back to me.

"It takes a truly mature, exceptionally attractive individual, with short hair, and impeccably tailored style, matched with a strong presence to tickle my fancy." Although I wasn't describing her pixie cut or exclusive Diane von Furstenberg garments, Mrs. Yumi found all the same characteristics in herself and assumed I was coming on to her. My close proximity to her body and gaze in her eyes made her highly uncomfortable to the point where she finally left me the hell alone and rarely made an appearance at the house, unless Stefan was home. She didn't trust me with her alone. Game over.

"I win bitch!" I whispered under my breath, in my room, under the covers, in my head. I still respected her, of course.

# sake to me

Coming out of a comatose state would typically prove to be mentally and physically difficult, but because of how my body healed, the return of consciousness happened swiftly. Customarily, I regained basic motor skills as if I was never without them. On this particular day, I awoke in a profound state of confusion.

"I was hoping you came to soon." My doctor checked my vitals like he'd repeatedly done for the last few months. He then presented me with a silver serving tray fenced with a dome cover.

"A gift for the gift." His ordinarily dry humor was still just as dehydrated and crusty as my lips were at that moment. I would have first preferred some water, or even some Vaseline, and THEN whatever was beneath the shiny lid. Possibly, he was surprising me with a cold glass of ice water with petroleum jelly glazing the rim.

"Voila!" Stefan revealed. Well, my hope for greasy lips was granted; it was a tray of bacon. As a health professional, he knew it wasn't the best source of nutrition, but as my friend, he rewarded me with the swine for my good deed of saving another one of his patients. It was never served up on a silver platter before though. Although we were in the morgue, his subtle sentiments were cute. It was almost morbidly romantic. I ate my bacon and inquiringly watched him while he wiggled my big toe and then wiggled my long toe. Was Stefan attempting to massage my feet?

"Um, thank you." I wasn't sure what was happening or how to respond; was he just completing my physical, or was he being physically affectionate? Either way, it was awkward. I hid my feet in socks and took my bacon to go. This little piggy cried what the fuck all the way home—to my room.

Unless I was sucking the life out of someone, or watching reruns of Good Times with my new best friend Mary, my days and nights primarily passed while I hid out in my room. I stalked those I left behind on social media to see how good or bad their lives had evolved or gone to shit. Somehow, I found gratification in comparing my borrowed house, money, and possessions to what I saw in their pictures. It was bullshit. I was bullshit. My existence wasn't entirely wasted though; I was about two hundred pages into just one of the enormous medical books from Stefan's library. The books coincided with the diverse forms of cancers I had ingested, and those I would ultimately consume. I thought it wise to train my brain, should I lose my free healthcare and in-home physician. I usually exhausted the first thirty minutes of each study session feeling confidently determined to soak up the knowledge. I then depleted any progress, typing every other word into the online Wikipedia trying to figure out what the hell I'd just read. Most of the unpronounceable terminology I sounded out made me feel like I was learning to read all over again. My approach to learning was an honest one; I comprehended what I could until my eyes crossed, said fuck it, and prayed something stuck. I played to my strengths:pictures. An entire wall of my room was committed to my episodes, the past present and future. The complex investigative drywall corkboard displayed pictures, index cards, thumbtacks and strings. I was just like all the detectives from the crime movies; I stared at it for hours hoping to make a connection as to what, when, who, and why me. My ongoing case might never be solved seeing as though I was both the perpetrator and the victim. I'd yet to give up though. Oneday, everything would make sense.

My studies were disturbed by the pacing of orthopedic shoes outside my door. My primary care provider wore them to prevent painful knees, hips, and bunions from his long hours in the hospital. The bodily fluids that polished them also prevented social interaction. I awaited a knock, but nothing. What was he doing; perhaps contemplating how to inform me that my premiums were going up? And just how did he expect me to pay? Camping outside of my door could have been misconstrued as creepy predatory behavior and ultimately ruled as a criminal offense. And if he wanted to sniff my panties, he should know I needed to do laundry. I opened the door.

"It's lovely to see you again, Chance," He nervously greeted me as if we didn't reside in the same house. His trepidation made what seemed to be stalkerish conduct, non-threatening.

"I was hoping you would be so kind to join me tonight at Sum Like Dim Hot?"

"I'm hoping that's the name of a restaurant and not some freak nasty porno you want me to watch?" I'd heard of the Chinese café before, but I found joy in making Stefan even more uncomfortable. He scrambled to explain.

"Oh no, I guess I never realized the sexual connotation or pun before. My apologies. I'd like to invite you to dinner where an assortment of steamed and fried dumplings are served." He made sure not to repeat the provocative name in his second attempt.

"Well, I usually don't give in to stalkers, but my self-esteem is extremely low today." I was comforted in knowing that he wasn't attempting to collect payment on the tab I had racked up. Frankly, there wasn't enough sex in the world to settle my rent, utilities, food, and medical supplies. My RSVP encouraged Stefan to kiss the back of my hand before he ecstatically skipped down the hallway. My relief curved to flattery. This wasn't just two friends breaking bread; he was crushing on me. I guess I never viewed him in that light before. I mean, sure he was attractive to the eye, but his dorky social awkwardness blocked any likelihood of me feeling him like that. He may have looked and sounded like Idris Elba, but he was Steve Urkel all the way.

Dressed in debonair civilian clothing, with his signature yummy scent altering the air, Stefan held open the door of his black executive car. I assumed his closet only consisted of scrubs. The distinctness in his makeover was appealing; like an old pair of shoes buffed with a little oil, he was made brand new. Me on the other hand, all I added was some soap and water to my ass in preparation for the night's event. I jumped in the luxury car in my sneakers, jeans, and habitual hoodie. Clearly we were an odd pairing. Oil and water were two liquids that were immiscible; I predicted a jinxed evening as we rode silently in the car.

"You look like you're holding in a fart." I broke up the silence amongst our table. Not that I was giving him permission to discharge his nervous gas, but maybe he'd release a few words. He exposed his lack of confidence from behind his menu to bashfully laugh.

"I do apologize for my sheepish demeanor. I'm shy, but not ashamed to say, your beauty throws me." It was the first time he looked me in the eyes all night. My dimples had never sunk so deep before, except that one time when I had lost a vast amount of weight and was dying. His introverted charm was growing on me.

"What you can do excites me. Your ability is beyond my intellectual capacity, and it's fascinating to watch you heal." He geeked out and turned me off in the process. It was within his amorous poem, that I realized he wasn't actually infatuated with me, but fixated on what I could do. Recognizing that you might be interested in someone in a romantic capacity should evolve naturally. With undeniable chemistry and common interests, the show and tell of your feelings becomes instinctive. Well, as immature and incompetent that I was when it came to the opposite sex, I could still distinguish the difference between sugar and artificial sweeteners. And as brainy as Stefan was, to him they were one in the same. He didn't like me; he liked my unique abilities that was directly related to his passion for his patients. I could play along and only hope to avoid a destructive wreck once he realized his misplaced feelings, or I could steer the train back on the platonic tracks.

"Two sakes please!" I adlibbed the latter; drunk platonic tracks just felt right. The Japanese wine snuck up on me and hit me like Bruce Lee. The eight sakes between us may not have been a wise detour, but the strong ethanol contents certainly diluted Stefan's goo goo eyes for me. My vision of the night blurred just the same. I couldn't remember if we ate, or the journey back home; I dim sum blacked out.

I walked a narrow wooden plank stretched out the window of the hospital's tenth floor. The weight of the endless white fabric that hung from my body kept me unbalanced. And the six-inch heels that sprouted from my Nikes made it even harder to progress without falling and landing into a sea of tumors. I tried my best not to look down, and slowly advanced to my guests who all sat in window seats sipping tea. My maid of honor, Olivia, danced to an eerie version of "Sexy and I Know It" by LMFAO; Ellen Degeneres did the running man beside her. I reached a man who, from the neck down, appeared to be Stefan, but the veil that shielded his face threw me off. It was androgynous and unlike him. The reverend Al Sharpton joined us via Skype and performed the odd ceremony before rushing off to wash the relaxer out of his hair.

"You are now legally bound to a world of oppression—you may kiss your husband." I stepped in close to peel back the veil. I uncovered a beautiful nightmare; it was Sophie. The crowd's laughter was so thunderous, like a jackhammer against my head. It jolted me awake. Through one of my heavy eyes, I found that the abrasive jackhammer operated by an inconsiderate construction worker proved to be Mary knocking on my door. I dumped my exploded head back into the pillows and played dead.

"Afternoon, Miss Chance." The vibration of Mary's voice was agony. I grabbed my forehead in an attempt to conjure up lucidness and also to ease the sharpness of my temples. Neither of which happened. Instead, Mary's movement triggered a disturbance in my stomach, and I raced for the toilet.

"You get wasted chocolate last night? Clean you mouth and meet me in kitchen." Mary insisted.

I eventually migrated to the kitchen where I slumped over the counter and watched Mary pour a hangover remedy.

"You drink." A glass of yellowish liquid was pushed towards me. When it looks like ass and smells like ass, it's a glass of shit. I kindly declined.

"No, you drink, girl gone wild." She unsympathetically placed the glass in my hand, poured the remaining contents into Stefan's usual orange juice wine glass, and went about her business. "Good morning, Chance." Stefan groggily appeared. Remnants of our lethal consumption still impaired him as well; disorientation of his eyesight shuffled the numbers of the clock. The morning had passed us by. Lack of toothpaste so late in the day assaulted the air, burning the hairs of my nostrils and poisoned the defenseless fruit that decorated the countertop. I slid the cure for his hangover (and more importantly, his hot knockout breath) in front of him.

"Thank you. Here, I got you something." Stefan presented me with a gift. It was in an already opened FedEx box, but presentation wasn't everything. Who would complain about receiving a Rolex watch in a plastic Walmart bag, right? But I had almost forgotten about the platonic pact we took the previous night, and clearly, he had too.

"Do you, by any chance, remember what I said to you before we got wasted?" I questioned before I peeked inside the box.

"You told me to never shit where I eat. Trust me, I got the colorful idiom loud and clear." He did understand my polite dismissal of his advances. So, should I open the package or not? After five seconds of contemplation, I, of course, opened it.

"Chance Yumi." I read what appeared to be my new name. Okay, what the fuck really happened last night?

"Is this some real-life Hangover IV shit?" I checked the fourth finger of my left hand for a ring, and I swiftly ran my tongue across my front teeth to check for elongated gaps.

"I figured you needed identification, a phone, and access to money. Regrettably, my pusher didn't have any Rohypnol," Stefan said with a smirk at my accusation. He went on to explain that Mary googled and found my photo on a missing person's site for the passport, the phone had unlimited data, and he'd allow me to charge up to two-hundred dollars a week on the credit card. His generosity was more than I deserved—espe-cially considering that I rejected him and accused him of slipping a date-rape drug in my drink. I felt bad, but not terrible enough to express regret—instead, I asked for the Wi-Fi password for my new iPhone. Stephan was a good guy, and one day I'd be able to express my gratitude, maturely.

"I'm going away on business for a few days. Maybe you'll go with me next time, for a change of scenery. Don't get in any trouble while I'm away." Stefan winked and left me to enjoy my new phone.

I finally gave in and agreed to go away with Stefan for the weekend just a week thereafter. It wasn't of the romantic persuasion, but we did join forces as a friendly dynamic duo. I followed behind his steps that guided me through the halls of Cancer Treatment Centers of America. Routinely, we targeted Stefan's patients and a few civilians here and there that kept us near the home front, but a unique case took our show on the road. We should have stayed our asses home. We traveled from Savannah to the state's largest city and capital, Atlanta, GA, where a teenage boy suffered from extreme loss of appetite and weight, an unceasing cough, painful swal-lowing, and even worse indigestion. His symptoms were a direct reflection of esophageal carcinoma; it kept him and his family hospitalized. Stefan let my hand go when we entered the elevator. Once inside, he reminded me of Peter London's room number and that he'd make sure his room would be cleared in exactly thirty minutes. The waiting area was a tasteless replica of a living room right out of the early nineties. The poor attempt to create a comforting atmosphere was less comforting and more confusing with the plastic plants, assorted furniture, and the subdued saddened faces of the paintings. I couldn't distinguish if they were created by true artists or self-portraits of the patients from the mental ward. I had no true productive thoughts while the minutes ticked. The details of our secret mission, that I chose to accept, were vague; Peter was the nephew of one of Stefan's colleagues. Stefan was to offer and provide a second opinion as an oncologist, and then I would swoop in to do all the work. We needed to seriously reevaluate our characters as it pertained to our capabilities; I was absolutely the Batman in this duo. Even so, I wouldn't let my ego self-destruct. I found my way to Peter's room; he was alone and asleep. I hoped I could have just aligned our faces, instead of adding my weight to his weak body. But he repositioned himself from laying on his side to his back, forcing me to do things the old-fashioned way. I moved quick, but with sleekness, careful not to wake him. I moved in close. He coughed, and the infected tube that ran from his stomach to his throat discharged blood on my lips. It was disgusting. Why didn't anyone cover their nasty mouths anymore—yes even in their sleep. I got on with it. The transfer of his disease supernaturally moved from his body to mine just as it should. What shouldn't have happened was the piercing pain in my side. The mist between us broke as I turned my head to the left of me and fell weak. I was in idiosyncratic belief, staring at Peter's solid spirit outside of his body, with a fork in his hand. There were two of them, with curly red hair and big noses.

"Get the hell away from my brother." Peter's twin brother took hostile action to protect his carbon copy. And as a result, I held droplets of my blood in the palm of my hand. Where did this little fucker come from, and where the hell was my sidekick Robin; it was the appropriate time to tag himself into the fight scene.

"Really kid, you stabbed me with a damn fork, you little silverware psycho! I was just trying to help your brother." I tried to defend my compromising position while the thirteen-year-old guardian parted his lips and sounded off. His ear-bleeding shrill was unplugged by Dr. Syringe. Stefan whipped out his weapon of choice and stuck him in the neck with a harmless venom that sent him straight to happy land. My newly-inflamed esophagus involuntarily made me cough incessantly, worsening my abdominal pain. Stefan propped the Chucky doll up in a nearby chair and pried the fork out of his dirty hand. He then ran out to grab our getaway car: a waiting wheelchair. He pushed me down the halls like a reckless shopping cart. Being young and reckless was supposed to be enjoyable; clearly, we were doing it wrong. I wasn't having fun.

"I don't think anyone saw us. I just need to clean your wound before we get out of here." Stefan was out of breath while he treated the four punctures in my side. He cleaned the area and added padded gauze and tape to seal the edges. I understood his urgency to stop the bleeding, because unfortunately my body healed from the inside, not the other way around. The river-dance of feet passing by our curtain made me nervous for both of us, but of course Stefan had more to lose. He patched me up and successfully wheeled me to safety.

We made it out of the volcano before an eruption. Stefan O.J.'d us home, and thank goodness our white Broncho went unnoticed by the authorities. My agony was coming from all sides, inside and out; I had never been so happy to see the morgue. We were so worried about putting me under that the dark and silent house went unnoticed at first. It wasn't until I awoke the next evening that I questioned, *where's Mary?*

"She's sick, resting in bed. She said she collapsed while we were gone—the doctor said she has gastroparesis. It's a stomach condition that affects the muscles of the digestive tract." Stefan gave me the abbreviated overview before leaving me to go check on her. My Google search gave me the particulars in full. The disorder was caused by damage to a nerve that controlled her stomach muscles, thus food remained in her stomach longer than it should have. The complications were hardened undigested food, severe dehydration, and malnutrition. I peeked in on her over the next few days and couldn't wait until her vomiting, abdominal pain, and bloat subsided; I missed my friend and a home cooked meal.

Leisurely mornings without concern past the border of a mattress was a privilege not offered to everyone; some never awoke, and most had no choice but to work themselves tirelessly into an early grave. I watched her as she was willingly stranded on the cozy isolated island, unconfined of worldly rubbish. Her sleep was peaceful. Despite the fact I stood over her bed like a black-cloaked grim reaper with unfavorable news, I envied her attractive mist of tranquility, so I climbed in bed with Mary and lethargically observed her room as she slept. Her living space seemed immaculately normal to the eye, but the random poster of Ice Cube threw me. How could a little old Hispanic lady conceivably relate to N.W.A.? It was strange, but she may have been from Compton and dated Eazy-E's daddy. Shit, who was I to judge her explicit choice in music? But I definitely raised a brow after pulling out a book with a sensuous cover flaunting two bodies placed in very challenging positions from atop her nightstand.

"Daily Dose of Intimacy—Advance risqué techniques and positions, secret fantasies, and erotic keys to unlock hour long orgasms. This book is filled with how-to's and illustrated guides guaranteed to savor intimate relationships 365 days of the year." I read the long title aloud. The brief interlude was enough for me to instantaneously whip open the super-hot collection and take a peek at a few of the full-color (and very demonstrative) photographs. Mary often shared stories from her collection of romance novels, but there was nothing romantic about this book. This was straight-to-the-point-fucking instructional literature. It was no modest Lifetime porn. The manuscript, and its thrilling possible positions, might have been deemed inappropriate in most countries. With my head vertically tilted to the side, my mind took an even dirtier turn, and I began to think about all of Mary's DNA on the pages of the book, quickly dropping it. I peaceably snuggled my head in her divine pillows and hoped she would soon awake so we could get on with it. Mary slept like she was already in the grave, dead to the world. Did the last grain of sand in her hourglass fall? Had the real bearer of bad news already collected Mary's soul? In an attempt to be proactive, I crawled on top of her.

"Wake up girl, it's time." Eventually boredom set in. I couldn't wait for this to happen naturally, I had important shit to do; The People's Court was coming on soon.

"Morning, Chance." Mary cleared the boogers from the edges of her eyes, and her groggy tone and hot, knockout breath assaulted my face.

"You're late for work, and a potentially terminal illness is no excuse for you not making me breakfast. Get up, and stop being lazy. But first you should absolutely scrub the decaying demons from your enamel before you meet me in the kitchen." I demanded that Mary do her job. It was hard to call in sick when you resided in your office building—no excuses. Mary was mentally in good spirits, but her physical body wasn't on one accord. Her legs moved at their own detached speed, heavily in stride towards the kitchen. I redirected her path to the dining room.

"Hello beautiful, please have a seat." I offered sweet greetings and a place for her to sit. I got up early and made Mary breakfast. I took pride in the preparation and execution of the feast by picking up the phone and placing an order for delivery from her favorite local restaurant. I made the delivery guy wait until I transferred the food onto decorative plates so he could take the evidence with him. I didn't need anyone to shed light on the empty plastic containers stuffed in the trash can.

"Oh my goodness, this so sweet." Her eyes filled with tears by the explosion of balloons, streamers, and confetti. Stefan appeared from around the corner with a single muffin lit with a candle; we sang happy birthday.

"What'd you wish?" Stefan asked knowing it was bad luck to tell. But I assumed it was something selfish like good health.

"I wished for you to find love," she responded to Stefan, but annoyingly grinned at me. She was better off wishing for Chris Brown and Rihanna to rekindle their flame; it was never going to happen. Stefan swiftly moved on to the gift giving time of the program. He presented her with two tickets to Jamaica for her and her sister. His gift was cool and all, but mine would outperform the materialistic and unoriginal present.

"Boring!" I dismissed him and stuck a big gold bow to my chest.

"What's better than me as your gift—oh, and the gift of continued life!" I threw my hands up in the air like boo-ya. Stefan looked confused, but me and Mary understood the significance of what I was giving her.

"Gastroparesis has very similar symptoms to cervical cancer." When I touched Mary that morning to wake her up, I felt it. I then went through her things while she brushed her teeth and found the official diagnosis. Why'd she attempt to camouflage it and hide it from us?

"I don't want you to waste your powers on me. It's for the children." Her self-sacrificing was noble and all, but shut up. Of course I was going to heal her; who else was going to cook, clean, and talk shit with me? It was going to happen whether she liked it or not. She was my closest friend at that time. Mary's tears of joy dried, and we all delighted in the celebration.

# i didn't know

once stumbled across a documentary series where the women were unaware that they were pregnant until they went into labor. I mean, how stupid could you be for the growth of a human being inside you to go unnoticed? Well apparently, I was stupid too. I wasn't in labor yet, but had just had an episode, finally relieving Mary of her cervical cancer when Stefan began running his usual tests before putting me under. The computed tomography scan was to evaluate the extent of the disease and detect if nearby lymph nodes were affected as well. His internal view of my organs revealed a developing embryo.

"Shit!" He was surprised. I don't think I'd ever heard him curse before, unless he was repeating something I'd said.

"You can at least wait to spy on my bowel movement when I'm unconscious. It'll be less embarrassing, jerk." I thought Dr. Yummy's use of the ultrasound was obnoxious, considering how much pain I was in.

"I'm spying on your baby." Stefan was my human pregnancy stick that I didn't actually have to pee on. He had to be a false positive. Feeling bloated and nauseated with a frequent urgency to pee were all signs of ovarian cancer. Additionally, a missed period, fatigue, and cravings were also tell signs that could have attributed to the disease—but now thinking back, those indicators happened before this episode. How could I not recognize the most common symptoms of pregnancy?

"Shit!" My mission to disappoint and slowly kill my mother continued; adding unwed mother to my bucket list was the nail in her coffin. Carrying a fetus while battling ovarian cancer might inadvertently be the death of the baby as well. This was crazy.

"Wait a minute…" My thoughts were chaotic and almost impossible. Was I a victim of immaculate conception? I'd never had sex before. Either I was carrying Jesus the sequel, or I'd sucked out more than just a tumor.

"Mary?" I questioned Stefan. His unconvinced expression confirmed that we weren't on the same page.

"Not the virgin Mary genius, but the Mary that lives upstairs, burns my bacon, and takes care of your house. The Mary who I just sucked the cancer out of—catch my drift?" I gave him several hints. We were finally on the same page. Stefan grabbed Mary's file and reexamined through her lab reports.

"No, there was no indication of offspring development." Stefan had no logical explanation. An illness, okay, but a fucking fetus? No way and no thank you.

"Mary!!!" I needed confirmation from the horse's pregnant mouth.

"Girl, are you pregnant or did you think you were pregnant?"

"I no booty call, you booty call." She denied the claim and insinuated that I called the booty. Her Spanish to English translation mostly formulated from black entertainment television. She'd watched so much BET, she listed Medea and Martin as her next of kin. She led us to Stefan's home office where she had a game of Candy Crush in progress, but she wasn't showing us her favorite pastime. Instead, she guided the mouse to the second monitor. She scanned through the folders and doubled clicked on a video dated two weeks prior. The footage revealed our normal daily activity—nothing special.

"Wait for it." Mary was that one person who already saw the movie, but devotedly wouldn't spoil the ending. The anticipation was killing me.

"Mira." She pointed her finger and told us to look. We leaned in close to the screen. It was me dancing through the front door, and what a terrible execution of the Wobble it was. Stefan stumbled in behind me with assistance from his driver. We both landed on the same decorative chaise lounge chair.

"What is this supposed to show us?" Stefan questioned. The inquiry was answered just seconds later. We all witnessed me straddle Stefan and suck his face. But not like usual; I didn't appear helpful, but aggressively horny. I was mortified and placed my hand over my mouth, but my dirty curiosity couldn't bring me to turn away or shamefully shatter the flat screen to pieces. Our clothes instantly fell off like an edited movie. I guess I was an alternative virgin. The kind who obviously had intercourse but claimed it didn't count.

"Oh shit!" We synchronized our reaction, among other things.

"That's enough." Stefan's wholesome voice com
manded.

"Okay, you the papi…and I clean." Mary fast forwarded to her on screen cameo. She walked into the shot
and one by one, she dragged out our drunken hot mess
bodies. She then returned to the scene of the crime with
disinfectant wipes. Watching it in rapid speed made it
kind of funny, but not everyone was laughing. Stefan
left the office. His face wasn't exactly joyous like the
men who couldn't disprove paternity to Maury Povich.

"Well, at least we don't have genital herpes!" I yelled
out after him. My look-at-the-bright-side optimism
didn't bring him back. The feeling of being a single
mother hurt; or it could have been the agonizing sense
of cervical cancer? My first duty as a mother:save and
label the surveillance as "Baby's First Video". My second
duty:don't die.

I found an inaudible Stefan back down in the morgue.

"A little help here, please." I was growing weaker and
weaker from the progressive cancer I'd just taken on.

"Oh please forgive me." He rushed to assist me, but
he was cold and avoided eye contact. I could tell he felt
culpable for our situation.

"Was that your first time?" Stefan was so cute wor-
rying about deflowering me, but that was the least of

his concern. His focus should have been on the seed he'd planted. I may not have been accidentally artificially inseminated, but in my mind I was still Jane the Virgin. I had no recollection of losing my virginity. So technically it didn't count, right? I surely didn't feel like it was taken from me. This was surely turning into an African American telenovela. The drama amplified with each new episode.

"No big deal, Doc. It's like getting the final punch on my Starbucks card—now I get a free latte macchiato baby!" I sucked at the optimism analogy thing. Somehow I made myself sound like a punch card coffee hoe.

"I respect you more than what we just saw. I would never unfairly impose myself upon you." He was taking it hard.

"I saw two drunken-hot-mess consenting adults." To most adults, at nineteen, I was probably still considered a child, and Stefan was only three years ahead of me. But mentally, due to his intelligence, and my old soul and partial hard knock life, we were the equivalent of two old fogies with a child already in college. Age was nothing but a number.

"We'll be okay—now get over it, and help me save our baby. It's probably not a good idea to put me under during this episode or any episode for the next eight or nine months, huh?" I was painfully correct. Stefan reached deep into the tiny crevasses of his brainy skull and tapped into his useless knowledge bank and regurgitated a page from a medical book verbatim. He enlightened me with facts about how medically induced comas were not recommended during pregnancy due to the possible birth defects, including, but not limited to: neurological damage and shallow breathing. He casually waited to mention miscarriage until the end. We agreed as parents, temporary relief of my pain didn't outweigh the risks. I waited for the cancer to pass naturally like the good old days: a vicious pain I didn't want to endure.

I had officially been profiled as CWP: Cancer While Pregnant. The conjunction of the two organisms growing inside of me was physically discriminatory, I couldn't help but be karmically offended. I must have done some seriously fucked up shit in my former life to deserve such pleasurous pain. While mild cancer itself hardly ever affected the development of a baby, I was still especially fucked because of my cursed condition. The possibilities of my complications were serious for both me and my health care provider, also known as my baby daddy. He was overly neurotic and multidisciplinary: do this, don't eat that, what are you doing smoking that joint? Stefan's definition of high-risk pregnancy and my reasonable interpretation differed. He confiscated the already rolled weed that I hoarded with me all the way from Kim's gingerbread house before I could even light up. I read various blogs that encouraged the natural remedy to treat morning sickness and decrease anxiety. I endured the discomfort, but declared that Stefan owed me one big fat doobie epidural the minute I went into labor.

The tumors vanished from my ovaries and eight grueling months of pregnancy began.

"What's this crap?" I made my revulsion known for the fruits, vegetables, and grains presented on the plate in front of me. My problem with healthy food had a lot to do with the texture, and the fact that kale and bananas felt nothing like ribs and doughnuts in my mouth.

"Doc says only well-balanced diet for healthy baby," Mary repeated the doctor's orders. Our obnoxious obstetrician was conspiring to annoy me and the baby. Here I was thinking the incubation of a tiny human in a continually diseased body would be the death of me, but then restricted calories and monstrous oversized prenatal vitamins moved in for the kill. The essential steps to bring forth a life made me question the sanity of every woman who did it willingly before me, but I followed instructions as best I could. Rule number one: Eat well, but not for two. Well that was easy. Ordering large Slurpees and "well" cooked triple stacked burgers was truly just for me. Rule number two: Watch my weight. I watched myself everyday as I wore sweatpants. No problem. Rule number three: Stay active. Regular exercise was against my religion, so I got down on my knees every day to pray away my developing back fat. Rule number four: Safety first. It was a little too late for that; we were unprotected first—duh! Rule number five: No chemicals. I minimized my exposure to hazardous elements by throwing most of the food Mary prepared for me in the trash. I never identified with those who acted in agreement or compliance; I was a rule breaker at heart.

"I have your lunch." Mary waited for me at the front door with a plate garnished with two hard boiled eggs, broccoli, and a banana; the grouping made me throw up in my mouth.

"Another lunch? I'm still full from the first yummy lunch you made for me," I lied with McDonald's chicken nuggets and fries on my breath.

"That's weird because I found that first yummy lunch in the trash can." Mary caught me, but I countered and tried to convince her that she didn't need to dig through the trash for food. She was better than that, and there was plenty in the fridge.

"Oh, I can feel the baby kicking. I should take a nap." I was overly dramatic seeing as though I was only a few weeks along; my embryo had yet to become a fetus. Blaming everything on the baby made my irrational conduct almost sane and excusable. I used the excuse every chance I could.

# couldn't hold my shit

I never imagined I'd find myself vigorously stuffing an obese genetically FDA approved chicken into a remorseless elastic garment, but I ate my words and everything else on the left side of the Popeyes Chicken menu. My reflection in the funhouse mirror exhibited a polished face and lengthy straightened tresses from the neck up and a bloated straw from the neck down.

"You look beautiful, Mami, but please change your shoes." Mary praised the hard work of a hired makeup artist and hairdresser, but disagreed with the footwear just below my cankles. I was more than half way through my eighth month of pregnancy, noticeably uncomfortable in a formal evening gown suffocating my stretched skin. My black dress was luxurious; the black chucks I paired with it, not so much. It was either sensible shoes or stay home. Shit, they're lucky I didn't just tie a bib around my neck and post up next to the lip-smacking display of hors d'oeuvres.

"You're perfect from head to chucks." Stefan weighed in with his adoration. He could have said I reminded him of a damn water buffalo, and I still would have replied thank you and accepted whatever gibberish he spewed. He was spellbinding in his single breasted black tuxedo, perfectly formed to his body. We checked our sexiness in the mirror, and what a fine non-couple we were. He then handed me a Venetian style half mask, which was mandatory for the annual fundraising gala, and we headed out to the event. The infamous all black masquerade enticed the wealthiest of the wealthy to get all dolled up and make obscene financial contributions for researching a cure for children's cancer. The bourgeoisie affair really wasn't my cup of tea, but Stefan insisted that I accompany him and meet all the donors who generously supported the patients who I couldn't save. Our accented sequined, beaded, and feathered faces colonized in the lobby of a grand theater. Everyone followed the instructions of their invitations and arrived in a mask, each uniquely decorated. The elegant scenery set the mood for a scene right out of Eyes Wide Shut: glamorously embellished with erotic undertones. I made sure not to make eye contact or connect with any other parts of the rich anatomy that strutted around the venue. Stefan ultimately left my side to spread his brilliance over the stale wafers. I too spread some fancy butter over stale bread and stuffed my pie hole, while I disingenuously smiled in the many faces. Why couldn't they all just forfeit the million-dollar, over-the-top affair and mail in their tax-deductible donations to help thousands of more kids? I guess the insanely rich couldn't just boast anonymously; they had to flaunt in each other's faces. It didn't take me long to abandon the over privileged semantics to search for the true purpose of my night; I had enough of the hardened crumbs. Where was the real fucking food?

I didn't speak to many people, but I made fast friends with the servers patrolling the cocktail hour. Our words were minimal, mostly due to the fact that I was just using them for the expensive food atop their trays— they proved to be loyal friends, because my mouth was always full. My chase of the circular platters ended, not because I was finished eating, but because the crowd migrated through the open doors of the theater. I was more than happy to rest my swollen piglets in the front row, inside the intimate and sensually garlanded auditorium that was truly reminiscent of a traditional opera house. Everyone sipped glasses of wine, while I flipped through the program. Images of Cirque du Soleil graced the pages; sexy characters wore more makeup on their faces than they did clothes. Now I had seen local productions of The Lion King and The Phantom of the Opera back home, but they weren't as seductively aggressive as this. I knew this was going to be some freaky shit. Rich people freaky shit. The plush cushioned walls, warm colored curtains, and grand winding staircases that absorbed the stage dimmed, giving the orchestra its queue to initiate the show. A fine sharply dressed black man appeared at the pinnacle of the winding staircase. He wore an impeccably tailored black Hugo Boss suit, black and white pinstripe oxford shirt, wrapped with a solid black satin tie and gray v-neck sweater. His suit pocket was assembled with a dotted handkerchief; the details were affluent, and he almost looked better than the man I attended the event with. The spotlight polished his mocha-flavored bald head and tracked every stylish stride as he fluently made his way to the base of the stairs.

"Good evening, ladies and gentlemen. I'm the president of the foundation that everyone is here to support, and of course, your handsome host for the evening." The confident lips that spoke into the wireless microphone belonged to Dr. Rick Holston. Damn, he was scrumptious; I could barely keep my legs closed—mostly because my legs refused to cross, due to the human that impeded my thighs. My belly hung unusually lower than the days before.

"I trust you left all your inhibitions at the door, because in this sinuous twist on veracity, there's no room for bashfulness. Tonight, we will take you on a naughty forbidden ride full of thrilling burlesque, cabaret, and acrobatics. Let loose and treat yourself to a night you'll never forget. Welcome to our provocative playground." Following his thought-provoking prelude, the stage went black, and the interactive orchestra traded their temperate vibrations for a thunderous sonata. The intense music summoned each character to the stage and the show began. The ninety minute show touched on the ominous face of eroticism with Kama-Sutra-enthused arrangements, tempting caged dancers, drag performers, gymnast, contortionist, and eye candy for both men and women dressed in risqué costumes. The surreal imagery was an intimate merge of dramatic avant-garde cabaret and circus-style acrobatics that told a story of peculiar comedic sexual ecstasy. It was undeniably entertaining, and I was overly aroused. I wasn't in control of my heightened sex drive thanks to pregnancy. My out of control hormones put Stefan at the forefront of my sensual thoughts. I wondered if he'd scratch my itch at the end of the night as a favor for a friend. I just hoped he took some notes from the show. Even if my belly would make some positions a physical impossibility, at least our second romp would be remembered. Dr. Holston ceased my dirty thoughts.

"I expect everyone enjoyed the show, as did I, so I'll make my closing short and sweet. The contributions collected over the years have not gone in vain. I'm delighted to announce that we have formulated a vaccine that is sure to piss off the pharmaceutical industry. Contrary to what most believe, killing cancer is not accomplished by killing the cells; it's achieved by reversing the affected cells back to their normal state. While other well-known foundations have no intentions of ending the epidemic, we have a natural cure for cancer in the form of a simple yet powerful pill. The battle is over!" Dr. Holston wrapped up the show with a revolutionary bow. The crowd stood to their feet with cheer.

We hung around after the show, not to socialize, but to wait for the other person who had the cure. I was curious and wanted a closer look; maybe there were freckles upon his face.

"What a great show, right? The performers are brilliant!" He greeted us: shook Stefan's hand and leaned in to kiss my right cheek. There was an aroma of dried liquid on his neck. Although tempting, it smelled less like the mesmerizing Escada and more like my next motherfucking episode. My stink face was unpleasant and impolite. I wasn't expecting to save anyone else so close to my due date.

"He might think he has the cure for cancer, but he's yet to cure himself—what the fuck?!" I whispered to Stefan.

"Oh no, it wasn't a good idea to bring you here. What do you want to do?" Stefan was ready and willing to flee the scene like he'd already mapped out our quickest evacuation route. What I really wanted to do was to be pushed around in a wheelbarrow filled with cheese quesadillas and maple syrup—but I guess saving the man who was confident in his abilities to save the world seemed more fulfilling than my weird pregnancy cravings. Stefan and I huddled for a brief private meeting: Bonnie and Clyde prepping to epically rob and kill cancer.

"And break!" Our game plan was set and the strategy was uncomplicated:catch him with his pants down. We casually hovered near Dr. Holston; Stefan kindly refilled his glass of bubbly until his inner cup runneth over. I followed the john into the john, whereas Stefan manned the door from the outside. I gave him space while he did his business and meticulously washed his hands, like only a doctor would. He caught my waiting reflection in the mirror.

"I'm all for equal rights, but you do know this is the men's restroom, right?" His look of confusion was two parts: why was a woman in the men's room, and why did she stare at him like a boxed combo.

"I have what you call an itch I need to scratch, and if you just lay down and take it, this will go a lot easier." In my measured movement in his direction, I must have tripped and knocked over my vagina. A huge gush of warm fluid slopped all over the floor.

"Look, no disrespect, but I'm not into golden showers or pregnant chicks. I'll see if I can get someone in here to clean that up?" Damn I couldn't even control my own bladder in front of the client; talk about unprofessionalism.

"Never mind that. I assure you, I'm a professional; I just need you to play along here. Are you aware that you have cancer?"

"Yes, but how did you know?" There was a surprised silence and then an admission.

"Well if you know, what was all the rubbish you were saying to the people about a cure? Why haven't you just treated yourself yet?"

"My tests have proven successful on the non-human persuasions: animals. I myself have failed as the ginny pig," he shared his defeat.

"I need you to keep pushing forward with your research because clearly you're on to something. And to help you with that, I need you to accept my donation. I can remove the cancerous cells from your body right here and right now, but we have to hurry because my cankles are killing me, and awkwardly I think my water just broke. I know this is some unorthodox shit, but please just lay down. Never speak of me or your cancer will return with vengeance." I probably could have left the warning part out; no one would believe his cockamamie tale of a pregnant lady who pissed herself before relieving him of his disease.

"Stefan!" I screamed for Stefan to enter the bathroom. I was gonna need his help.

"Whoa, why are you all wet? Was there a struggle?" Stefan swooped me up, cradled my weakened damp body in his arms, and carried me out like a scene right out of The Bodyguard, or any other notable movie where a man sneaks his baby mama from the scene of a crime so she didn't have to give birth handcuffed to a bed.

The third most commonly diagnosed cancer in men and women is colorectal cancer. I wanted to send Dr. Holston a thank you card for giving me his destructive abnormal cells that wasted no time going haywire in my poopshoot. I'll save everyone the gory details of the magnificent combination of pushing a watermelon through my keyhole and an extremely nearby malfunctioning rectum. Fast forward—born six pounds and three ounces, we called our newborn baby girl Fate Lynn Yumi, and then we promptly called a hazardous waste company to expunge the imageries and smells of the occurrence from our minds. With such a bizarre beginning, motherhood was destined to be fucking fascinating.

Stefan was a fond and efficient father. His patient and gentle embrace in the early mornings and late night, before and after his rounds at the hospital, soothed Fate and calmed her clear hatred towards me. This was one more thing boy genius excelled at. I was envious—turns out I was a terrible fucking mother. Not Sophie terrible though. My mother was so cold, she gave me goosebumps. But not the good shiver pimples; it was the bad kind, like herpes. Her affection was infectiously painful. I didn't plan to pass the same virus onto my child. I wasn't sure what I expected, but it was evident that I was terribly lacking in the territory of child rearing responsibilities. I mean, my love was innate, but my gag reflex for shitty diapers and baby puke was not. According to the one parental manual I had skimmed over, I was considered detached—which was total bullshit. I disconnected my phone from the charger, not my tit from my child's mouth. My adaptation may have been slow, but I was so overly connected that I wanted to contact all those mothers who made motherhood look and sound so easy to attest—what a nice, big boiling crockpot of shit! I was a sleep deprived lunatic with raw nipples and raging hormones. Having a healthy baby should have been my reward. Nope, a nice cold crisp bowl of Cocoa Puffs was the only satisfaction I looked forward to. It'd been two weeks since I indulged in the artificial chocolate yumminess; I was overdue. While the parasite slept, I took the eight and a half minutes I had to refill my body with milk covered cereal. I sunk my exhausted body into the couch with my bowl in my lap and remote in my hand. I shoved the huge silver spoon into my mouth and disregarded the dripping milk down my chin. The white dribble would fit right in with the rest of the dried up crud that found refuge on my body. The first luscious crunch into the processed grains sounded like a nuclear bomb to my baby girl's ears; her panic-stricken eyes jacked open instantly.

"Way ahead of you, you cute lil' monster." I moved Fate from the left side of me where she laid on her tummy to the right side of me to prop her up on a sleeping baby pillow with a pacifier. In the transition, the stump of tissue that had dried and shriveled up finally detached from her belly button. I'd been overly cautious cleaning the area for the past two weeks and what was left of the ugly crusted umbilical cord plopped right into my long-awaited bowl of puffs. Even an individual with an otherwise sound, but questionable mental function, who is burnt out and sleep deprived could succumb to all the external stressors that fall into their cereal; a mental breakdown was unavoidable. Putting the baby down before I pulled all of my hair out and turned cuckoo-for-cocoa-puffs was the responsible thing to do, but just in that millisecond, she puked and added her regurgitated breastmilk to the mix. I needed a fucking intervention; I was unsure of how I'd react if I wasn't rescued.

And just beyond the ocean of turmoil, there stood my archenemy waving a white flag and seemingly offering help. Her stretched arms were like a flotation device to my drowning stability. By now she knew I was no longer, if ever, after her lady parts. Could she have been there for revenge and possible kidnapping? I did what any sane mother and matriarch would do: I allowed my child's deranged grandmother to rock the cradle, while I abandoned my mommy duties and ran for the hills. No words were spoken, just a mutual understanding between enemies to call a temporary truce. Although I found it difficult to ask for help, or accept it when Stefan and Mary offered, in that moment I gave up all my parental rights for twenty minutes of personal space. I cried the baby blues, and my somber call for reinforcements didn't summon the sanest candidate, but Fate and Grandma Yumi could search for her marbles together for all I cared. I ran to my room like I was being chased by a bull. First things first, I washed my nasty ass. I was ashamed to admit that I couldn't remember the last time soap became one with my skin. I rested my head back on the smooth, acrylic, clawed tub, comforted the lids of my eyes, and hummed a familiar melody. It was a Brandy song that I couldn't quite put my finger on. The lyrics escaped me, but the wordless tune emerged from my cords with coolness. The benefits of soaking in the tub were amazing; it reduced stress and anxiety, decreased tension of headaches, diminished body odor, and most importantly, it improved my sleep. Regrettably that sleep came immediately. My relaxed body easily glided amongst the comfortably warm bubbles and eventually submerged into a nightmare. Water flooded my nostrils; the panic and disoriented mental alertness made me think I was being attacked by some mythical boogie man. The spasmodic breaths pushed the suds into my windpipes. I flailed around like Nemo until my breathing and reflexes returned to normal and realized my psychological realism of Freddy Krueger was imaginary. I may have been cleaned, but I was more distressed than before. Fear helped me to abandon my soothing immersion. With one foot on the polished travertine floors and the other attempting to exit the bathtub, I slipped and unwillingly found myself in the splits. I had never done the splits in my life. In fact, the only time I'd ever come close to so severely stretching my vagina was when I gave birth. This was worse. My flexibility and patience for finding peace were both being tested beyond repair. I omitted rubbing my body down with lotion and tenderly crawled my ashy ass to my bed. If there was one thing to bring me serenity, it would have been Netflix. It provided an addictive escape from the outside world with endless streaming of Stranger Things and Pretty Little Liars.

"What the fuck?" An error popped up on my iPad. I couldn't catch a break. I needed something to make me feel good, and in that same thought, my phone vibrated the sheets.

"I found a new case for you!" It was a text message from Stefan. Men sure did know how to pile on the shit sometimes. My maternity leave just started like two seconds ago, my vagina was still stretched to my knees, and he wasn't psychically inclined to recognize everything I needed without actually telling him—how annoying. I cleaned my room, ate some snacks, watched a fly bounce around the walls, and I antagonistically yanked the long hairs from my chin. Mommy time proved to be a waste; I felt unfulfilled and incomplete. The faint cries of Fate drew my concentration. At first, I didn't move to help, but eventually I couldn't take it. The thing I was trying to run from was the very thing I needed for that sense of satisfaction and fulfillment. I went and got my baby and we laid in the bed together. In the end, I couldn't sleep without Fate next to me. We both slept like babies—that was until my pulsating freckles pulled me from my fantastic dream into a tangible nightmare. My anguish was so loud, Fate awoke also. It was time for us to feed: me on someone's cancer and Fate on my tits. Why the hell didn't my curse offer maternity leave?!

# who heals the healer?

A constrictive chest pain made for an irregular heartbeat and shortness of breath. On the verge of collapsing, a severely weakened body drooped over the bathroom sink agonizingly coughing up mucus. Barely conscious, two heavy weighted eyes sluggishly rose and met the mirror. By now, my concern for such familiar symptoms was nonchalant. I found relief in knowing it would soon pass, like a violently delicious burrito. But on this day, the fragile reflection was not my own.

The doctor calendared the expiration of Stefan's life three months from that day. That day, the doctor became the patient: poked and scanned and branded with an expectancy of death due to advanced congestive heart failure. Advanced was just a pretty word for terminal. But what was the point of putting a bow on a pile of shit? It was still shit. He sympathized more than he dwelled on the details of hospice; the doctor didn't need to explain to Stefan how this would play out. Stefan had sat in his seat many times before, delivering such devastating news.

"You are family to us here at this hospital, and we're here for whatever you need." Unlike Stefan's colleague, I was unable to offer attractive expressions of support. I was overwhelmingly concerned for myself.

"Please say something," Stefan begged for communication, while I selfishly sulked in silence. If I verbally acknowledged he was dying, I'd have to admit that I couldn't save him: a debt I undeniably owed to him. Talk about life giving you the middle finger—Stefan jam-packed his heart with love for ailing children so much that it was bursting at the seams and literally killing him.

"I wish you had cancer." It was a lousy thing to say. Repeatedly knowing first-hand the ramifications, I wouldn't wish the illness on my enemy, but my power couldn't fix a broken heart—mine or his. He wrapped his dying arms around me, sharing my same fears; he wouldn't be around for his daughter, his mother, or me.

There was no right or wrong way to cope with end of life affairs. The rollercoaster of emotions were warranted, but placed on the back burner to make sure his mother would be cared for, his finances were assigned, and that his daughter would appreciate and benefit from her daddy's legacy. I didn't crowd him. I allowed him to live out his days how he wished. I even pushed my episodes until my self-absorbed freckles would no longer stand to be ignored. I didn't want to miss a single day hearing his accented voice, or seeing his unbreakable smile. The times he wasn't on the phone delegating for his estate, he enjoyed the sweet scent and laughter coming from his baby girl Fate. I got my time in when his body wouldn't allow nothing else, but a soft nap; I stared at him from afar feeling useless. I served no true purpose; he asked nothing of me and barely spoke most days . I guess I was okay with being low on his importance pole, as long as I still saw him every day of those ninety days. Graciously, those three months were prolonged, in spite of the ill-fated prognosis. Stefan continued to cheat death a year later. But his mood that initially appeared somberly sane swung severely to the complete opposite end of the mental pole—but in a good way. While his swings were pure comedy for me, for Mary, they motivated her to walk off the job.

Ordinarily, Stefan was a pleasure to cater to—his sincere smiles and the pleases and thank you's he shared as gratitude made it feel as if Mary was just helping a dear friend. A new medication to curve his weak depressed disposition had an adverse effect on their relationship. Stefan's stellar gentleman's charm for the entireness of his life proved to be very two-faced when he locked himself in his master suite for two days and callously demanded his meals through the door.

"You're late, and I'm hungry!" Stefan barked when he opened the door and allowed Mary to enter on the third day. Inside, Mary boiled from the insolence, but her exterior kept its cool.

"Hello and good morning, Mr. Yumi?" Stefan posed the question, expecting that that's how Mary should have greeted him. Her attention was on the disgusting mess he'd created: days old food scattered about, a shattered mirror and orange juice sprinkled the floor, and the air held an unventilated rotten stench.

"Mary!" Stefan's patience was thin. His new dramatic character reengaged her attention. Deceptively, they were actors in an impromptu performance, where Stefan starred as the condescending monarch, and he portrayed Mary as the dim-witted peasant. He may have been dying, but I feared for his life— if his tone didn't soften, Mary would take her theatrical stance as a psychopathic nurse swinging a sledgehammer at his ankles. Misery was in her eyes as she stepped over the evidence of an unhinged man and placed the tray of coffee, bowl of cheerios, fresh fruit, and two slices of buttered toast on the floor next to the bed. It was the only uncluttered space in the entire dysfunctional scene where it would fit.

"Why the hell would you put my food on the floor, you idiot?!" His vicious mind didn't allow him to see that Mary merely placed the food on the floor until she could clean a reachable surface.

"Ay dios Mio…you ungrateful motherfucker!" Mary exited stage left, refusing to continue as a caretaker, custodian, and compassionate friend.

"Get your ass back here." Stefan jumped up from his filthy sheets and tried to follow her, but stepped his bare foot right into the bowl of cereal.

"Bitch!" He threw the slur right along with the spoon and bowl out the room. The mental patient look went well with the cheerios dripping from his toes.

"You're gonna pay for that, my dear," he cynically sang into the air. This saga was better than any drama series I'd ever watched. Mary furiously buzzed by me where I noisily observed from the hallway. I stopped pretending to just be walking by, and I entered his world. I knew exactly how to get Dr. Jekyll to Hyde his evil and cruel dual personality.

"I'm going to run you a bath and get you cleaned up, while Mary prepares another meal for you," I lied. Mary was on her fuck you train blowing off steam. I knelt down beside the tub and adjusted the spout to release a hot stream of water. Some candle therapy and Epsom salt would relieve his obvious tension. The added dim lighting set the ambiance for a drowning.

"Alright, I'll leave you to it, and I'll be back with a surprise." I'd never seen Stefan naked, that I could remember; I gave him his privacy. I re-entered his master bathroom with two special guests: Fate and Bruno Mars. Bruno gave us some 24k Magic, and baby Fate jumped around her father who was submerged in the large modern spa tub. She found the rhythm of the music more engaging than anything else. Well, I assumed she was dancing; she mostly just stomped her chunky feet, and I did witness her raise her tiny pinky ring up to the moon. Fate's ecstasy melted Stefan's heart as he blew bubbles from his bath over her head. The diversion gave me time to find his newest prescribed medication and drown the bottle's evil contents down the toilet. The new chemicals introduced into his body may have helped one thing, but sent him deeper into a state of aversion. The hideous side effects were stealing the natural euphoria of his numbered days. We sang and danced until his body was soggy and our cheeks hurt from smiling.

The house was peacefully quiet one Sunday morning. We all just lounged around doing nothing in particular when wisdom spoke out.

"He loves you, you know? He just thinks it's easier on his heart if he pretends he doesn't—which is pretty dumb for such a smart man who knows how the entire body functions. You two seem to be operating on the same braincell." Mrs. Yumi was a woman of few meaningful words and hadn't really spoken to me since around the time her Poli lost its grip, and I showed superficial interest in her. She rocked back and forth in front of a luminous window, throwing enlightening shade. I wasn't sure that my feelings of being ignored were real or selfish until she confirmed that they were both; Stefan was keeping his distance, and I was too.

"He's just like his father. He's going to push you, Mary, and me away because he thinks we'll be too busy hating him to miss him. His father did the same to us when he knew he was going to die. It's stupid, but I understand now. And it won't stop me from loving his seemingly hardened heart more than ever—I made that mistake once before. I replay those days of my husband with death on his tongue. I should have kissed him instead of feeling sorry for myself. Losing the men of our lives is only a loss if we allow it to be." A single tear finally escaped from her heart through her eye. Damn, perhaps she wasn't crazy, just hell bent on giving her son the love she feels she denied to his father. Maybe it was my turn to stop feeling sorry for myself and express how I truly felt. I finished listening to wise counsel and decided to check in on Stefan.

"Stefan, it's me," my voice gently requested to enter his room. Following no response, I awoke the door hinges, peered beyond the entry, and quietly entered. Stefan rested atop a deep quilted comforter, his head effortlessly afloat the feather filled pillows. I tread tenderly to the left side of the king-sized display where I could see Stefan's face, his eyes sealed with dreams inside. I never laid in his bed before, and I regretted those days and nights gone by. I climbed on the embellished fashioned mountain and rested in the vacant space next to him where the early morning rays pushed through the shallow blinds and warmed the air. The soft essence layered Stefan's face like an illuminated self-portrait. Given that he could awake at any moment and catch me being creepy, I was still. As I quietly admired, I witnessed moisture develop in the tiny creases of his eyelids. A single tear broke free, skimmed over the bridge of his nose, and disappeared into the fabric. Maybe he knew I was there, but was just too weak to react. Were they tears of joy, pain, or regret I wondered. I wondered if it were even me who engaged his thoughts at that very moment. I magically placed myself in his dream and convinced myself that it was time to tell him of the love I'd clandestinely held for him over the time we'd come to know each other: a sensitivity that only pushed to the surface once I thought he'd no longer be there. Driven with an optimistic mutual reaction, I turned over and aligned my back against his chest. Delicately, I grabbed his left arm and wrapped it over my waist to cuddle me.

"Stefan." I was sure to have woken him. But when I pulled his arm tighter, he didn't hold on. Maybe he wasn't pleased: not only with my entry into his room, but my forced affection. Too little, too late. I didn't intend to shy away, but his stubborn ass wouldn't budge. Not even a word to banish me or movement to push me away. I slightly turned my head back over my left shoulder in puzzlement of his rejection. His stillness was absent of inhale or exhale. I soon realized his lack of affection wasn't personally directed towards me; he was incapable of physically showing me emotion. Stefan was dead. My eyes clenched tight, to the point of pain. My heart raced and beat on my shirt. My breaths became heavyweight and bottomless; they were uncatchable. Every strip of fibrous tissue that wrapped my body was rendered powerless, too petrified to even move. The tightly woven blanket that we laid upon slowly unraveled.

"I'm not ready to lose you, Stefan." I selfishly whimpered, knowing my cry would go unanswered. He was lifeless. I lived on the edge of death hundreds of times too many, but I had never been so invested in someone who had actually verified imminent demise and gone over that edge. And although paralyzed to a sensible reaction, I couldn't just lay there in fright. My scared and immobilized body awakened, permitting me to quickly slide from under his limp arm, and I scurried off the side of the bed. Panic rushed in while I searched for a phone, and the simple task of calling for help was nearly impossible.

"Please help…need an ambulance, he's not breathing," I conveyed with shaky hands and broken babble.

"Okay calm down, miss. Tell me who he is and what happened?" The emergency operator tried to make sense of my devastation. I couldn't dare utter the damaging sequence of letters that was his name or that he was dead; they rang too destructive to my heart. A stiff silence blocked the line of communication. My mind and body became unresponsive to the extent of a withdrawn stupor. The traumatic scene appeared to slow around me, just like my very first episode with Olivia's comatose body; only Stefan wouldn't come back to life. The phone was snatched from me.

"His name was Doctor Stefan Yumi, and he is DNR. We'll await your arrival, thank you." Stefan's mother took over the call. She was calm to the paramedics and coroner whom all seemed to fade in and out with every sluggish blink; our reactions should have been reversed. My daze spanned about an hour and a half long, but it felt outside of time, an infinite blur.

"Da Da!" Fate's language development progressed just in time to distinguish her daddy's love, so much that she searched for it excitedly that day. It wasn't her innocence that broke me down, it was her soothing baby kisses and hugs that comforted me when she saw mommy hurting. It relieved me that he would leave her remembrance just as fast as he arrived there. I held on tight and rocked my security blanket to sleep.

# narcs & narcotics

My knowledge of funeral preparations stemmed from brief, fictional scenarios I'd seen in almost every dramatic, morbid movie. These movies didn't just want you to know someone died, they wanted you to witness their body in the casket, big ugly flowers, darker than dark attire, and an intense organ playing their outro music. Good thing I wasn't on the planning committee, and Mrs. Yumi had every over-the-top detail arranged before I could wipe the Viola Davis snot from my nose. While she worked intensely as a coping aid to numb the sensation of grief, my quiet somberness lightened and a need for loving warmth was at the forefront. The warmness rested peacefully within a dream. I climbed in Fate's shrunken bed and hungrily pulled her close in my arms to reassure the tiny beat of her body still produced a loving percussion. The passion of my cuddle woke her and her gasses; she farted on me. Flatulence wasn't the warmth I sought, but I took it and giggled.

"It's time to get ready, baby." I brushed her teeth and perfected the tight curls of my princess before dressing her in the all black ensemble sent to the house by Grandma Yumi. She was in formation with the excess of two hundred relatives, close friends, and associates that journeyed through the massive cemetery, each with a flower in hand. Their somber faces silently gathered around the burial ground I imagined. Statistically, I didn't know how often a death at a funeral occurred, but an impromptu death at said funeral was redundant. I didn't intend to add one of my episodes as a shocking party trick. Yeah sure, I had mastered the art of restraint, but using my unique illness as an excuse was the easiest way to mourn privately and catch up on the new season of Luke Cage in peace. Besides, homegoing services were nothing but slow walking, loud crying, endless Kleenex, and fucking depressive bereavement. There were two types of people in the world: those who want to feel the pain and those whom numb it. I absolutely intended to numb it one way or another.

My smoke-filled chipmunk cheeks were frightfully deflated when someone banged on the door—it was the feds politely knocking before they busted down the door in search of the single joint I'd smuggled from Kim's grow house years ago.

"She dropped a dime on me!" I frantically fanned the clouded air with my open hands while trying to quiet my chronic coughs. I felt like my half a joint was the equivalent of a crack house, and I was about to be raided. My guilty feet softly crept to the door's peephole. The fisheye view showed an overweight middle-aged white man with no badge nor army behind him. What I thought was a controlled substance instigated a lack of control; I was a recreational wreck. I even pulled my hoodie over my head as if it were a magical cloak that would make me invisible. I was experiencing paranoia at its finest.

"I know you're in there. I can smell the weed. Open the door." His tone didn't enforce the law, but his creepy old pervert demeanor screamed stranger danger. I wouldn't be surprised if his name was Chester and he drove a white van.

"Sophie Dubois asked me to find you and make contact." He exposed himself as a private investigator, hired by my mother of all people. How the hell did they find me? I had protected my travels, strategically hidden amongst the deceptive world like Waldo.

"Find me for what?" The threat decreased, but I spoke up with apprehension.

"Look lady, I was paid to find you and deliver this envelope. She didn't exactly share her heart's desires with me. Please just open the door, I only get the rest of my money if I put this in your hands."

"I'm allergic to human interaction. You're not sick, are you?" I couldn't think of a more inconspicuous way to ask and warn him not to touch me should he perhaps have cancer or any other creepy man disease. Weed had a funny way of clouding my supernatural judgement. My ordinary skill of restraint could fail; finding myself spread-eagle over his pop belly on the front porch— that was not an option.

"If obesity and alcoholism classifies me as sick, then yes." Curiosity raised my cat whiskers, triggering a distinct area of my brain: stupidity. I opened the door with only my gnawed on claws to protect me.

"Thanks." I took the manila envelope. Chester's nosey self delayed his departure. It wasn't clear if he expected gratuity for services rendered or was interested to know what he'd been carrying around. We played the who would blink first game. He did.

"Got any more I can have for the road?" He gestured his fingers to his lips as if he were smoking. He appeared less of a professional and more of a panhandler. I shut the door and ripped open my delivery.

"If you're reading this, my efforts and prayers were successful. I've missed you dearly and would love to lay eyes on my baby girl again. I respect your wishes to remain private, but should you want to return, if even for a day, I've enclosed cash for your travel arrangements. Anytime is a good time. Your brother and I anticipate your homecoming. I love you." Sophie Dubois personalized the message with her initials. Was it possible for a gargoyle with saggy tits to be reformed into a sweetheart? The letter oozed of sugary bullshit. My mother had never expressed endearment without an audience. I wasn't sure what to make of it. Weighing the pros and cons of returning home proved to be challenging, due to the psychedelic journey my mind had taken. Getting stoned opened my brain's creativeness to euphoria of impractical likelihoods. I was in a genius conversation with myself in favor of chartering a private jet and simultaneously acting as the pilot, passenger, and flight attendant, all while waving a banner out the cockpit window that read "salted or plane deeez nuts?" I made myself laugh. As I flew amongst the clouds of ultimate mortality, my flight crashed on Sophie's lawn, and my argument against my initial views was now far out paranoia met with cancerous zombies. Much to my surprise, they only wanted to accompany me to the nearest bodega for chips and soda. Our relatable munchies surmised an obese truth—the world was a scary place, but I left my favorite pair of retro 13 Jordans in my bedroom years ago; it only made sense to go home. I vowed to stop smoking that day.

There were two tasks I needed to accomplish before leaving: suck the cancer out of someone and meet with Mrs. Dawn Powell, per one of Stefan's last desires. I checked cancer off my list, no problem. The meeting on the other hand, I didn't know what to expect. Fate and I sat unsuspecting in Mrs. Powell's office. Fate counted her dolls plastic fingers, and I counted the passing minutes, impatiently hoping that Stefan's attorney wouldn't keep us waiting much longer; we had a plane to catch. Plus, neither I nor Fate could sit still for long; adulting was so boring. Finally, the door knob turned.

"Hello, Granny's baby." It was the queen of Zamunda in her Coming to America floor length fur. What the fuck was Mrs. Yumi wearing? I didn't realize she'd be joining us, and in all her quirky luxuriousness no less. The four seats became occupied and we began.

"Not only was Stefan a great friend to me and my family, he was unquestionably a genius in every aspect of his life." She took a moment to saturate a tissue with tears and then restored her professionalism. She began to read.

*"Please excuse me. He wasn't just a celebrated physician, he had also mastered the art of financial reproduction. I know, Mrs. Yumi, you have recollection of his father's wealthy family tree that was essentially chopped down with taxes and public probate to about sixty grand, the family mortuary and an adjoining single family residence. The inheritance was mere pennies in comparison to the blood, sweat, and tears his grandparents endured while laying the foundation for what was ultimately estimated as a multimillion dollar estate. I can assure you that, morally, I am nothing like those previous greedy attorneys who pissed on their client's graves, no offense. Knowing firsthand the scrutiny of government seizure and temporary social demotion, Stefan took his legacy, tripled it sixty times over and worked overtime to protect every single investment. As such, as his long time legal advocate, we prepared a family trust distinctively structured to benefit his most precious assets; his mother, daughter, mother and guardian of his daughter, and closest friend. Fate Yumi has been listed as the sole beneficiary, Anita Yumi and Chance Yumi are listed as co-trustees, and I've been named the executor of the estate. My title doesn't entitle me to any effects outside of my normal attorney fees, which have been paid in advance. My job is to make sure that you understand and abide by Stefan's wishes*

*in maintaining the estate, and in doing so, you'll receive your portion of the small empire. Said empire includes, but is not limited to, his primary residence, the vacation home in the Hamptons, a condo in Washington state, one 2010 BMW X6, all rights and future profits from his bestselling medical books, although not in operation, full ownership of Yumi Mortuary, and all cash allocations in the sum of twelve million dollars disbursed over three bank accounts, two interest bearing savings accounts, and a trust fund in Fate's name. Outside of the million dollars that will be donated to three separate charitable foundations, the assets will be divided as follows: Anita Yumi will remain at the luxury assisted living facility, and her expenses are covered for the remainder of her life, with an additional monthly stipend in the amount of five thousand dollars to be deposited to a debit card in her name. The property in the Hamptons will be sold, and the net profit will be forwarded to Anita in one lump sum. She can also choose to keep said property for personal use. Mary Rodriquez, who is not present but has a separate reading of this will scheduled immediately following this with a Spanish translator, is the new owner of the primary residence located at 1981 Brook Lane to be shared with Chance and Fate Yumi, should they choose to stay. Her current salary shall remain in place as long as she continues to maintain the property. The BMW has been placed in her name to use as she wishes. Chance Yumi, also known as Chance Dubois, will raise and protect Stefan's only child with a monthly support stipend in the amount of ten thousand dollars. She can remain at the primary residence, should she choose to. The property in Washington will be sold and the net profit will be forwarded to Chance in one lump sum. She can also choose to keep said property for personal use. Fate Yumi will receive her trust fund in the amount of three million dollars the day of her eighteenth birthday. Yumi Mortuary has been placed in her name should she choose to one day take on the family business. Fate, Anita, Chance, and Mary must meet for weekly dinners and take a family trip once a year. If any party of this will and trust refuses to keep Stefan Yumi in their hearts and minds, said parties forfeit all rights to the assigned assets."*

Dawn looked up and met our eyes. Our new full-time attorney and trustee handed Anita and I copies of the will, our debit cards, her business card, and she shook the hands of two extremely rich women and a millionaire toddler. I felt something when our palms touched, and it wasn't rich. I wondered if Mrs. Powell felt it too—or if she even knew she had cancer. I contemplated helping her, but I wasn't going to save her. Not because money had changed me, but because I had two non-refundable first-class seats on a plane that was scheduled to leave in a few hours. Nope, cancer could not and would not consume our lives; Fate and I were entitled to a small vacay. I wasn't a total asshole; I left her with a telepathic diagnosis. Fate and her grandmother stretched their legs in the hallway.

"I'm something like a disease specialist or diagnostician, and you're exhibiting signs of abnormal cells. Sorry to be so blunt, but if no physician has told you yet, I believe you have cancer." I probably seemed like a lunatic medical Nancy Drew, given that she looked at me like I were insane. I gave her a piece to her medical puzzle, but it was up to her to further solve the mysteries of the symptoms she'd been ignoring. I would move her name to the top of my to-do list once I returned to ensure the lady who divvied out our money was alive and well for years to come.

# déjà voodoo

The Louisiana sun peeked inside the window and kissed our unconscious skin. The warmth woke me. It was a perfect day to finish thawing downstairs in the courtyard of our charming rental I found on AirBnB. Linked to our unroofed botanical patio was a vintage café, just steps from Bourbon Street, which provided the perfect morning blend of breakfast and a show. People watching in the historic neighborhood, that was comfortably nestled in the heart of New Orleans, was more than pleasing. The familiar spirits relaxed my soul. I was happy to be back and eagerly scanned the assorted cluster of people whom heavily roamed the bars, restaurants, souvenir shops, and the all-important strip clubs. There was no formal parade of Mardi Gras, just an endless line of hot messes that apparently felt that 9 a.m. wasn't too early for the unreserved to flash the nips beneath their elaborate metallic beads. I was hungover just watching them. I had to admit, I was one of those old ladies who get their jollies by spying on others, clos-et-ly entertained by shameful, worthy mischiefs.

"What'll it be?" our waitress cured my hangover. She stood before us in her casual uniform complete with jeans, company t-shirt, a stained cotton apron that tied in the back, and a white plastic identification tag that read "Chakakhanna." Her name was just as ghetto as the gum smacking in her mouth.

"What'll it be, princess?" I questioned baby girl who sat across from me, elevated to her knees of the black cast aluminum chair to make her petite existence known.

"Some gum?" Fate stared at Chakakhanna's smacking mouth in all envy and seriousness. I giggled, however Chakakhanna wasn't as amused. But what did she expect? She made it look like the tomato soup, roast beef, and baked potato flavored gum invented by Willy Wonka. Shit, I wanted some too.

"We'll have two sweet teas, scones, fruit cups—oh and bacon please," I didn't really need time to review the nasty ragged menu; I ordered according to what was stuck to it. I bypassed the dried syrup, eggs, ketchup, hash browns, and everything else served over the weeks.

"Sorry no bacon." Rejection in life can be painful, but the refusal of bacon was just downright blasphemy. With disdain on my face, I substituted our favorite meat for cubes of deli ham. "Mom, some gum!" My greedy little girl was persistent.

"I want some too, but she doesn't want to share, and secondhand gum is not on the menu. Or maybe it is." I joked as Chaka Khan's love child rolled her eyes. Our every woman server dissolved her fake smile and left our table. I sent up a quick prayer before our tea and pretty little nibbles arrived in an effort to eliminate any of Chakakhanna's personal mucus seasoning.

Our food arrived and my less-than-tranquil child managed to monopolize our mealtime conversation— that I could understand any of it though. Never-ending toddler babble kept her lips busy; it was a wonder how she finished her finger food and tea. I requested the bartender cut her off from the sugar stuff. I ordered her a shot of water and for myself, a shot of adult reality: coffee. Fate lured me into her wonderland, deep in the rabbit hole where her imaginary friends included Doc McStuffins and Zendaya. My child was just as peculiar as me. I detached from her fantasy world and scanned our airy surroundings. Just beyond the steam from my cup, a wrinkled face wanted desperately to join our already crowded tea party. Usually when you catch someone all in your business, they quickly turn away, but this lady gave zero fucks. She gawked intensely until I gave her my undivided attention, to which her deep-rooted finger summoned our company. What was this chick smoking? If she had something to say, she needed to get up and put those Tempur-Pedic shoes to work. She eventually came over and uninvitedly sat down across from me. We sat in an eerie silence while she made a visual inspection of me, and I only felt it fair to do the same. She was seasoned, both physically and mentally. The thick silver strands that matured from the roots cascaded over her assured shoulders and coated her arms and back, and the time taken in silence to evaluate me and our happenstance implied wisdom: a virtue I'd yet to acquire, since I was two seconds away from asking what the hell she was looking at.

"Hello." My manners or fear of being slapped by my elders weren't too far removed, so I politely began. The ends of her mouth elevated creating a smile: a familiar expression. She raised her left hand to scale her scarred cheeks before she verbally reacted. She was fascinatingly calculated.

"A second chance paints a spotted face." Her statement held a veiled meaning, and I couldn't untangle the conundrum. Was she speaking in tongues or in Dr. Seuss?

"I do not like green eggs and ham. I do not like them, Chance-I-am." I sarcastically attempted to solve her riddle.

"Ya sharp tongue just might cut itself one day… Sophie's girl." Her thick Jamaican accent countered my witty remark with caution and disclosure. She knew me, she knew my mother. Triggered by this new key piece of information, combined with minimal prior knowledge, I experienced an epiphany.

"Ahh the urban legend…Sophie's mother." The sudden realization helped me to connect the dysfunctional family dots. I'd never encountered her before, not even so much as a photograph, but recognized my mother in her. The family resemblance was no longer an uncertainty. I heard few tales and could only speculate that our deviation from the norms of social behavior originated from her. I mean, why else would my grandmother be exiled from the very family she produced. I expected grand enlightenment to make sense of all that my mother refused to share. She didn't deny my suggestive identity of her. I continued.

"Sophie told me that my grandmother thought I'd be better off aborted." I skipped through the long story and got right to the other tea—since we'd both emptied our cups.

"Is that what my evil chil' told ya huh? I know ya wasn't conceived in love, but for a selfish motive—or as she call ya: a second chance. So yeah, I guess I didn't approve of ya conception, but it's too late now right? Ya here." Her lack of shame was as strong as the black coffee that stained her teeth.

"A second chance for what?" The curiosity to know the dramatics behind my given name was killing me as I readily anticipated her response.

"I know ya left, and I know why ya left, but how'd she get ya to come back?" She answered my question with a question, to which I wasn't sure how to answer. How could she possibly know why I skedaddled? And it wasn't clear that Sophie got me to return; maybe it was of my own volition. This lady was an alleged connoisseur of my business, or had magical powers of her own.

"She brought ya here for a reason, ya know? Maybe not for a convenient family reunion, but for a cancer." Oh she was good. It was like she was trying to inform me without informing me. We both showed impassive expressions, all the while our poker faces got fiercer by the minute. It was strange, like we were playing an intense game of Clue.

"I know how ya got ya gift, or depending how ya view it, ya curse." She authoritatively captured me. More, more, I needed more. But my long lost grannie was suddenly also lost in thought. Her mannequin challenge or senior moment was noticeably convenient to my brother's entrance into the cafe. She spoke no more.

"You shouldn't keep company with the senile and insane." My brother's intentional disrespect and disregard for our grandmother flowed so natural all the while with a smile on his face. I met his stretched arms with warm embrace. I hadn't seen his big head since the day I left —I missed him. I also missed the episode of his extreme makeover. A fitted black suit over a crisp white shirt, embellished with simple black tie, and shades was a huge improvement from the broke down pimp look he faithfully fashioned. From superfly to secret government agent, he was Will Smith in Men in Black.

"And who is this?" Anthony released me from his bear hug to inquire about my tea party. I turned around to see that half of my guests left the party early. Sophie's mother disappeared. I introduced my older brother to my baby girl.

"What a unique name. What's the story behind it?" Anthony inquired. I shared the cute rehearsed version: she was destined to be here, beyond my control. It sounded a lot better than I didn't remember what happened because I was a drunken whorebag one night, and technically I still consider myself a virtuous virgin. Anthony was too mesmerized by her pure eyes, big bouncing curls, and little human sweetness to even really care about the meaning behind her name. She trapped many unsuspecting adults that way: hypnotized until she released grown-up-sized dumps and challenged all authority. He'd soon snap out of it.

"Why so much hate for our supposed senile and insane grandmother?" I probed Anthony during our car ride to Sophie's house.

"Mom told us the stories about Hazel. You know she's crazy." Until he mentioned it, I couldn't remember Hazel's name. Clearly, he was fed more than I was; he even recognized her on sight and hated her as if he'd known her personally.

"Actually, neither of us know anything first hand—we only know those stories," I played devil's advocate.

"You're too young to remember, but mom struggled for years from the pain her mother caused her. She used to lock herself away in her room for days at a time. That should be enough for us to pick a side and stay away from her." My brother still fed from our mother's tit; he still followed her close like a shadow. It was hard to distinguish which one was Pinky and which one was the Brain.

"So, what's up with your new GQ style?" I changed the subject.

"Mom formed a new business of executive bodyguards a few years back. I still have all my old digs, but now I just dress the part of a CEO." He was proud of himself, and me of him.

"I even carry a gun." Anthony took one hand off the wheel to expose the holstered firearm on his waist.

"I hope your training to use that thing was more extensive than just endless hours on your video games?" We laughed as we approached the familiar historic neighborhood. I admired my old block before entering the house. Nothing much had changed in the Dubois home, except now a terrifying Egyptian mummy sat in our kitchen and sipped her breakfast through a straw.

"What the fuck?" I intended to greet Sophie sincerely, with a self-assured aura of maturity; I reverted back to the crass unfiltered daughter she last remembered.

"My foul mouth Chance is home." Sophie, in true form, didn't rise to her feet to welcome me. Her traditional rudeness didn't shock me, it was the fact that her entire head was wrapped in bandages, to either preserve her decaying face, or solidify her recent plastic surgery for her selfies in the afterlife. I told my face to smile, but my expression was one big question mark; she looked crazy as hell. It was a bit awkward.

"Oh, no need to be scared. I just had an aggressive chemical peel." She tried to explain away the mounds of cloth as she sat still in her tomb.

"Hello, sweet precious baby." Sophie's overextended arms did request the embrace of her granddaughter though. I knew it was my mother underneath the mask, but my poor little Fate saw a bootleg ghost; she fearfully hid behind my leg. A woman approached Fate with a single chocolate chip cookie.

"This is Denise, our housekeeper." I initially thought Denise to be Sophie's submissive lover the way she stood there all pretty and mute; that would have actually been more accepting than finding my mother solitarily mummified.

"Maybe she'll warm up to me once she sees all the pretty gifts I will have for her next time I see her. Oh my God, I can't believe my baby has a baby. I'm so happy you're home—come sit with me. How are you, what have you been doing all these years, and how old is this wonderful grandchild of mine?" Sophie's interrogation was underway; I had a hard time taking her seriously, given she was dressed in her Halloween costume and all. I had memorized a full account for my whereabouts, but the original story of simply running away somehow escaped me. Some cockamamie lie about being on a religious sabbatical came flowing out like diarrhea.

"I was doing God's work." It wasn't a total fabrication of the truth; I was saving lives. I just wasn't the typical willing servant, joyfully rescuing men and women from an afterlife of torment and demons. I was an abnormal, unwillingly-vexed slave rescuing men and women from their current life of torment and disease. I guess the two weren't so unalike. But I surely wasn't going to try and explain my role in the method of repeated suffering and healing. And I hoped Sophie didn't bring up the past: the disguised miracle she once witnessed with me and Olivia. I wanted her to forget about what she remembered, even though I constantly relived it. I went on to share limited details about my time away and hoped it satisfied her.

"I reached many sick children of God on my journey, from the streets to the hospitals, and all were healed. I even preyed over The Rock one day," I told no lies. And my famous encounter was a nice touch.

"That all sounds lovely, dear. So, why didn't you bring your bags in out of the car?" Her contentment with my vague answers, but inquiries of my luggage was suspicious.

"We're staying in a room downtown," I answered.

"That's silly. Why wouldn't you just stay here? Denise made the guest room up for you." Usually the houseguest is the nuisance, but in this projected horror, the host would make me very un-fucking-comfortable. I declined.

"You'll stay here. Anthony will go get your things and check you out of your room." She was used to giving demands with no backtalk, but I wasn't a child, and I damn sure wasn't gonna suck her tits like my grown brother.

"I said no thank you." I preferred to sip the mimosas Denise placed on the table over Sophie's spoiled milk. Her eyes pierced between the gauze.

"I paid for your tickets home. The least you can do is stay your ungrateful ass here in this house with me, with your family." Sophie gave her authoritative directive. I quickly noticed that the two of us may have matured in age, but our toxic dynamic was still the same. She was still a bitchy snow queen with icy temperament, and I still delighted in pissing her off. That's when I reached into my shoulder bag and pulled out the envelope with the money she'd sent.

"We flew first class." I slid her coach money across the kitchen table, reneging on her no-strings-attached gift. I wondered for a half a second if I was too old to get my ass beat by my mother. I wasn't ashamed to pick up Fate for a quick hug and, most importantly, to use her as a human shield. My mouth may have been arrogantly grown, but I was no fool.

"How about she just stay for dinner Mom?" Anthony inserted himself in the rising battle; he would have been safer just getting his phone ready to record our throw down for evidence of the homicide. His brotherly attempt to offer an alternative was appreciated. Dumb, considering our mother might literally cut his dick off, but appreciated. I downed the mix of orange juice and sparkling wine, savoring the inebriated calm before the storm.

"I've made plans, but thank you. If we're able to return for dinner, I'll call Anthony to make a reservation." I had a feeling our composed interaction was about to turn into a Love & Hip Hop reunion show where all the feuding guests planned to settle their battles with their fists. I trusted my vibes; visiting hours were over. I gathered my child and left the Dubois manner. We could try again another time.

# my spirit found its animal

"Olivia!" I felt like my left butt cheek had been reunited with the right the moment I saw my unicorn. My best friend is what I missed the most; she was the fat to my back, the love to my handles, and the dozen doughnuts on my cheat day. Our car pulled up in front of the address she'd texted me. Olivia waited wildly for us.

"My lesbian lover!" She left the man who she shared a union with on the porch and ran to me: her first love. His face questioned his marriage at that moment.

"I have missed you so much. You just don't know." We wrapped our arms around our obese love and held on as tight as we could. We released each other long enough to abandon our children with Olivia's husband, and we ran away together. We sprinted right into heaven.

"Hello ladies and welcome to the Elite Touch Spa. I am Katy, and I will be your specialist and will ensure complete satisfaction in your three-hour cleansing, healing, and rejuvenation experience. If you will please follow me, I'll guide you to your first treatment." Katy was a young, enormously energetic lady who probably pissed rainbows and butterflies. She wore a white, logoed uniformed top, simple ponytail, a hint of lip gloss, and a light flowery fragrance. Her sweetness was infectious and her certified ass kissing absolutely rubbed me the right way.

Between our two kids, and just a hectic life in general, we were obligated to have our every necessity catered to. Olivia and I were led to a haven of sophistication where we stripped down to our bare essentials, and Olivia's nipple ring, and we wrapped our skin in thick plush bathrobes. I adjusted the belt to a comfortable breathing liberty and fine tuned the generous collar to a cozy fit. Our taste buds indulged in Riesling and chocolate covered strawberries, while we anticipated the manipulation of our muscles and tissues. Katy's million dollar smile reappeared, and the three of us shuffled our feet over the six thousand square foot European spa that graciously offered steam rooms, saunas, facials, massages, a full salon, and much more. Olivia paused to peek in a cracked door.

"Stop it, that's a private room." I slapped her on the wrist and pulled her back in line. I invited my crazy comrade to enjoy a day of pampering, not to peep at naked people.

"What? I thought I saw boobs." She shrugged her shoulders. Olivia hadn't changed a bit. We continued on our course, passing slate walls with cascading water features as our sugar-filled consultant gave us the inclusive particulars of our customized package.

"Your individual baths have been drawn, and a fresh glass of wine will be served as soon as you submerge. Oils will gradually be added to your water, and the process will increase perspiration, as well as detoxify the skin. Soak, relax, and enjoy." Katy temporarily removed her perky lips from our backsides and left us to absorb the rich minerals. We disrobed and melted into the silky therapeutic oils and just as Katy promised, a fresh glass of white wine was served. With bubbles up to my neck and steam saturating my face, I exhaled. My mind was uncongested and my mood was set at a steady relaxing temperature—that was until Olivia tampered with my personal thermostat.

"So, what's going on with you? Where the hell have you been girl?" She couldn't wait to catch up. I went through every single detail and gave an account for every day we were apart, even my French kiss with a dirty ass rat.

"I have to admit that I moderately doubted you back then and that's possibly why I let you go so easily that day; I thought you'd come back once your mythical make-believe world got old. But there's no doubting your beautiful freckled face. Tell me how it works. How do you choose who to heal? How did you choose me?" Olivia wanted to know why her, but I wasn't sure why her. She was my first, but not by choice; I explained how my abilities were far more advanced than when it began. But being able to pick and choose was probably worse than not having a choice at all.

"Thank you," Olivia said after hearing my entertaining story. Gratitude wasn't exactly the response I expected, but I interpreted it as a thumbs up from my best critic.

"Wow, I had cancer. I didn't even know I was sick. You healed me first…thank you." She again expressed her gratitude and I then understood; she wasn't Siskel & Ebert, she was alive & grateful.

"Hello again, ladies. I hope you enjoyed your baths. Your personal helpers will now collect your glasses and provide you with fresh towels to dry off. Feel free to continue in the secure body towels or your robes, and I'll be waiting right outside these doors to escort you to your next endeavor." Katy exited the room, and two women helped us out our tubs safely.

"Next endeavor, huh? I mean don't get me wrong, this place is unbelievable, but I can walk around my house naked, drink wine, and take baths for free. How much is all this shit gonna cost us?" Olivia inquired.

"Today is on the late, great Dr. Yumi. Well, technically it's on Fate, who recently became a millionaire." It was weird to say aloud: both referring to Stefan in the past tense and accepting that we had more money than we would ever need because of him.

"What?! Well in that case, we'll take a bottle of champagne and another tray of chocolate covered strawberries, please." Olivia made our money hers too.

"Yes, little Miss Fate Yumi is the sole beneficiary of her father's estate. I beg for a few coins here and there for, food and shelter," I said, causing us to giggle.

"Allow me to introduce you to our professional, highly skilled massage therapists. They're here to perform a variety of specialized techniques to loosen up the tense tissue and reduce physical and mental stress. Please choose a table and convey your preferred points of contact, and your therapist will cultivate your neglected areas from head to toe. Enjoy." Katy vanished, and everyone communicated their wants and needs to their personal therapist just as instructed, and the hands on action began. Maybe we should have started with the massage portion of our package, because the knots of my stress were definitely affecting my attitude. I articulated the recent stress I'd been feeling throughout my entire body, but requested my therapist to pay special attention to my lower back. I buried my head and laid exposed to the stimulating fingers and hands that manipulated my tight muscles. The deep, amazing intensity put me in a numbing condition, and my ears were the only functional elements on my body.

"Awww, I wish my husband would give me this kind of treatment. All I ever get from him is a damn headache." Olivia pleasingly moaned as her therapist catered to her hands and feet.

"Why'd you come back, other than to see my beautiful ass?"

"I'm not quite sure how Sophie and her detective found me, but it just seemed like it was right on time, given Stefan's death and all."

"They probably saw you on YouTube, like I did. At first I wasn't sure it was you, but then I recognized that same ol' black hoodie you used to always wear. A few fly away curls peeked out from your covered head. I'm glad you traded in that antiquated goth look for…well, I guess your style is still dreary—would it kill you to wear some color, some sunshine? You should hire me as your personal stylist with all that new money you have." My best friend was never impressed with my style choices; the nonchalant tomboy look still left her unenthusiastic.

"Can you find it for me?"

"Yeah I'm sure I can find boobs and a vagina in there somewhere," she tickled herself before doing what I actually asked for. Olivia passed me her iPhone. As soon as I looked at the frozen screen I was embarrassed and reluctantly pressed play. When I first moonlighted as an Alabama vagrant, I found humble accommodations on an isolated farm. I slept on barn hay and ate fruits and vegetables from the crops. I hoped that when it was time for an episode, that I would find myself atop the sweaty physique of the long haired cowboy farmer. Devastatingly, he was healthy as a horse, and his actual horse was plagued with cancer. Just my fucking luck, the actual stallion had an uncontrolled growth of masses called lymphosarcoma, and the farmer had a high definition camera phone. He caught the whole awkward exchange on his damn cell phone and posted it online; how the hell did he get cell phone service all the way out in the boonies anyway?

"I actually originally found it on horsewives.com, but it wasn't until someone leaked a blurred version of it on Youtube that I noticed it was you." She later explained that she wasn't intentionally surfing the web for videos of humans having sex with animals; she inadvertently typed horse instead of house. I skeptically took her word for it.

A jolt sent vicious electricity from my foot up through the center of my body; clearly I was experiencing a vivid memory of being kicked by that damn horse. It was one big voltage of agony that made me drop Olivia's phone.

"You ticklish?" A robust Russian lady found delight in making me spasm as she stroked the nerve endings in my feet.

"Excuse me miss, can I get one of those happy endings too, please?" Olivia desired to end with painful pleasure as well. She sounded more than frustrated, sexual or otherwise.

"So, tell me about James." I was excited to learn how different our lives turned out.

"James who?" She pretended to be unaware and then made it clear that the man she may have shared a child and home with was not a shiny trophy that she cared to show off—James was not invited to our spa day. I got the feeling that maybe James used to send shock waves up and down Olivia, but the thrill was gone. I left it alone.

"I should have run away with you—your world is definitely an exhilarating, juicy tale. Mine, on the other hand, is dryer than my vagina." She envied the good highlights, short of truly recognizing or understanding all the bad. I gave her the there-was-no-gift-without-a-curse mantra—blah, blah, blah. She was fascinated by me, and I was bored of myself.

"You're more than welcome to come back with us. Our kids could be best friends, grow up together, and we can be Oprah and Gayle again. You just let me know when, and it's done." One month in my twilight zone, and Olivia would be begging for her old, usual life and dry vagina.

"Oh, 'cause you got all this money, you automatically think you're Oprah huh?" She always made me laugh, and she was right—I was Oprah damnit! Our massage therapists incorporated both warm and cold stones down the centers of our backs, compelling us to simmer down. A calm came over our dialogue, but only for a minute before Olivia posed a very compelling question.

"So, if you're Buffy the Cancer Slayer, then who is your dad supposed to be in all of this—you ever thought that maybe he has some answers for you?" Olivia's insightful observation made me giggle and then think. Who did my father resemble in my little fucked up fairytale besides just a ghost dad? I paid the $682 bill and sent Olivia home in an Uber, to host a sleepover for our little girls, while I went to go explore my roots.

# daddy wasn't there chronicles

As I came within steps of Milon's house, the sidewalk was warmed by the light pushing through the custom drapes. The unforgiving curtains exposed an abandoned silhouette of my father, and the open window gave the street's bystanders a free, inebriated show. His attempt to unify his common voice with a popular song that echoed the English crooning of Adele was almost unrecognizable; I'd reluctantly attended this karaoke concert limited times before. What I remember of our relationship, although inconsistent, was pure, so I didn't harbor any daddy-wasn't-there hostility towards my so-called absentee dad. I always knew his physical and financial absence had less to do about his efforts and everything to do with his controlling baby mama.

Sophie's shady methods benefited no one, but herself. My few memories of him all included the dying cat stuck in his throat and, oddly enough, it was endearing. As charming as Milon was, he was also miserably flawed. After evening hugs and kisses, I used to slip from my rainbow sheets and quietly watch his self-loathing party for one from the top of stairs. I'd witness his one manageable glass of rum recklessly measured. And that single glass was heavily poured (ten times too many) when he mistakenly allowed memories of love lost to take control. His heart ached most for Sophie Dubois. Their passionate affair, although extremely short, produced only one good thing: me. He was an underprivileged, free-spirited lame who couldn't hold a financial or social candle to Sophie's exclusive lifestyle. I'm not sure what he saw in my mother and vice versa. Maybe she found unconventional liberties in his raw, untrained world; unfortunately, the two pennies Milon rubbed together never sparked more than a restricted booty-call. Sophie got me, and Milon got a new best friend manifested in the shape of a bottle. I felt bad for him, being the only one in his audience. I entered the living room and took a front row seat to witness him in his most vulnerable state: drunk, singing relatable blues into an invisible microphone.

"Said I love you…more than you'll ever know," he croaked. His feet moved with slow simplicity to the dark, jazzy melody; impersonating Donny Hathaway's unique diction and dramatic intensity.

"My angel is here!" He paused his karaoke concert to show love to a fan. Shocked to see me again, he fanatically kissed my cheeks.

"You've grown into a beautiful woman. You look just like your mother with all those glorious freckles." He celebrated my strong resemblance to Sophie, an alikeness I never knew existed.

"Sophie has freckles?" I couldn't remember a time my mother ever shared a single blemish with the world. She lived and dreamed with flawless skin. With a picture frame pulled from a shelf, Milon danced with it in my direction. There she was with a spotted face, and my reflection fit seamlessly. Deceptively, she lived and dreamed with flawless foundation.

"Dance with me, my love child." He invited me into to his miserable realm where his five o'clock shadow was five years overgrown and whiskey was worn as cologne.

"How can I go on, dear, without you? You took the part that once was my heart. So why not take all of me…" Billie's timeless ballads were so relevant, blanketing my dad's face with tender tears.

"I love you, Dad." I suspended his cries and forced a smile on his face. He grabbed his glass and danced in my direction. I didn't mean to crash his invitation only party, but I'm glad I did. However, I didn't come to sing and dance. I stopped his soul train and sat him down. I hoped he had pieces to the family puzzle.

"Why'd you stop coming to get me?" I questioned.

"You're the best thing that ever happened to me baby, but your mother thought the worst of me. Something about she had to keep you safe; as if I would ever risk or jeopardize my restricted time with you. It was like she wanted to keep you in a fucking bubble. The convenience of a wealthy mother, and the inconvenience of a poor father whose love was bigger than his wallet, persuaded a family court judge to eliminate the small grasp I had of custody. My heart was ripped from me twice; I just don't have any luck with you Dubois women. You know, I only even found out she was pregnant with you because of a nurse who thought the father should know." He shared more than I ever thought he would. His integrity would never allow him to speak against Sophie, but the liquor-infused truth serum he'd ingested had him squealing like an episode of *The First 48*.

"Sophie had this crazy hold on me, like I was under a spell. I did whatever she wanted, but it wasn't until you came that I challenged her. She told me that if I fought for you, she'd ruin my life. And she did just that. My business crumbled, I was arrested, I lost visitations, and the love of my life." He was gradually giving me solid details, and then abandoned his confession.

"Get up and sing with me, my love child!" He insisted and I, of course, joined in. It was our first visit in over fifteen years.

"I came in like a wrecking ball!" The next song in my dad's playlist sounded oddly familiar. A fifty year old man singing Miley Cyrus was my cue to go.

"I've got to go, Dad, but I'm gonna come back and spend more time with you. I need some real estate advice; maybe we can invest in something together. How does that sound?

"That sounds great, Sophie," His intoxication mixed me up with my mother when he called me by her name. Even still, he kissed my forehead, leaving behind a wet impression of his favorite top shelf liquid. In retrospect, I should have stayed longer...danced more, sang more, made my trip home more about him and less about Sophie.

"Goodnight, Dad." Our farewell, although genuine, hurt. He didn't even know I was there and, more than likely, wouldn't remember me in the morning.

I returned to my Airbnb and found judgmental comfort in observing the lively streets from my window. I pulled a chair close enough to kick my feet up with a chilled glass of my favorite mix of 7UP and grenadine. The French Quarter was vastly different once the day disappeared; the clothes became less as the drinks were consumed in an effort to drown each liver. Bourbon Street was notorious for sleaziness; it was better than tv. The loud music and flashy tourists kept me entertained. It was a welcomed distraction from the strange family tree I was discovering—or at least I thought. There she was, an old branch amongst the freaky forest. While scanning the eccentric carnival, Hazel just stood there watching me watch her. The squint of my eyes only made her face become even more vague amid the commotion, and then she disappeared. That was the second time she pulled that Houdini shit on me. I grabbed my shoes, phone, bag, and ran out onto the drunken streets after her. She couldn't have gotten far, but seemingly, her sandbag ankles moved like Usain Bolt.

"I hoped we'd cross paths again. It's me, Chance. Am I crazy or did you want me to follow you? Can you please stop? Hello." I sounded like a perverted purse snatcher asking for permission as I ran up behind her. She didn't acknowledge my acceptance to her silent invitation though. I must have gotten the come-down-and-talk-to-me signals mixed up. She ignored me, oozing a mysterious and bizarre vibe. Nerves and clammy fear filled me, but I followed her anyway…right to the boundaries of the street that met the darkened Louisiana bayou; good sense wouldn't move my feet any further. It was pitch black, with pending horrors beyond the unknown. My ability to make sane decisions was questionable at that moment. What the hell was I doing? I mean, how well did I really know Hazel: my so-called grandmother. She could be just as crazy as Sophie and Anthony said: a psycho, murderous axe-splitting old betty by night and a sweet civilized member of AARP by day. I wasn't ashamed to admit that I was afraid of the dark. Furthermore, blood wasn't thicker than my fear of her haunted cabin in the woods.

"It was nice to see you again. Bye Granny," I called out to the creepy air. I went into stranger danger mode and wished her a good evening.

"Nothing can harm you, scary girl." Hazel reached back and yanked me into Narnia. The deep shadows helped my mind to race with uncertainty of the lurking evils. A mysterious crawling sensation on my exposed calf made me the loudest monster out there. Once I finished my erratic chicken dance, I looked down to see that it was just an innocent brush with a manicured shrub. It was part of contemporary and pristine land-scaped grounds. How did we go from a chilling swamp to unique decorative stepping stones, metal planters, and perfected flowerbeds? My fairytale-induced mind thought sorcery, but it turns out our few steps amid humble trees was just a shortcut to her luxury down-town apartment building. I expected a shabby shack with dead chickens hanging from the ceilings, jelly jars of eyeballs, and fattened children cooking in the oven. It was the complete opposite, I walked right into the reveal of a HGTV renovation show.

"Umm, what is it that you do again?" Naturally, I was curious to know how she afforded to be on an episode of Cribs.

"Investments." She was vague.

"Like real estate, livestock, cocaine?" I needed to know the specifics of my inheritance; would I be a tycoon, a farmer, or Nino Brown?

"Like Louisiana Powerball." Investor was an incon-spicuous way to describe herself as a lottery winner. Must have been quite some jackpot. I sat at the high marble countertop that allowed me to watch as Hazel shuffled through the kitchen cabinet that housed her

All-Clad silver cookware. I waited for our exchange to commence, but she made little noise.

"So, are you to blame for my mother's bullshit parenting or what?" I took on the role of Wendy Williams and initiated the hot topic. She temperately shook her head up and down as if to agree to disagree and eventually verbally replied.

"I lived with a bully fa' many years. Their disgusted glares and insensitive words were cruel an' hit deep, beyond me fleshly deformity. These lesions on me face were caused by discoid lupus erythematosus, an' having that disease increased me risk of developin' cancer. Me adult insecurities, although high, were no match for the evil, lil' child. The combination of the two left me a wide open target for mockery. This overbearing person, who habitually shouted how weak and ugly I was, had absolutely no compassion for what I was going trew. They were ashamed to be seen with me an' blamed me for me own sickness. Their fixation on tormenting me was more agonizing than me actual illnesses. I was physically disfigured, sick, an' plagued with verbal persecution…one had to go." Hazel shared her horror. My grandmother's surplus of pain pushed to the surface and spilled from her eyes as if she still lived in that egregious moment. Bullying wasn't just an epidemic with my despicable generation, it's been rampant and wide-spread from decades past. I remembered the uninspiring single paper handed out by our school that explained how they strongly frowned upon physical and verbal acts of bullying. The inside of the four corners failed to mention critical elements of prevention, so I wondered how one who is bullied would have defended themselves. Who could they tell their American horror stories to with hopes of protection?

"So what did you do?" I wanted her to continue her fascinating story.

"I was hated by the one I loved the most, an' their hatred came from lack of empathy an' lack of understanding. So, I made them understand." She turned her back to set a pot on fire while she kept me in anticipation. She dropped in miscellaneous elements, stirred, and continued.

"Our Creole roots run all the way to me mother's mother who introduced me to traditions of spirits an' worship of our ancestors. I used to watch her perform a ritual with a crucifix, amulets, candles, a bowl of ground-up ingredients, an' the most powerful commanding words. It was a ceremony intended to evoke protection." Granny was intense. I read of voodoo once, but never thought I had any tangible relation to it, or gave it actual merit of realism.

"In a moment of retaliation, I mimicked her ritual… but I unleashed me own personal commanding words. I wore her inherited crucifix, burned candles' an' I combined herbs, root of a tree, an' drops of me cancer blood into a bowl. I called on me ancestors to allow me tormenter to not just understand me pain, but feel it an' see it in them self. And for the rest of their days, their compassion would be so powerful that the weak would be restored.

*I reflect the harm that is placed on me*
*Let evil eyes see beauty*
*And wicked words replaced with sympathy*
*Attract the pain of the weak for one day for eternity*
*A mark upon your face will be your loving reminder*
*That a cruel soul should be remorseful and kinder*
*Bind the dark heart and negativity of the child I call Sophie*
*Protect me with light and love—so shall it be.*

I repeated the incantation over and over before putting the spellbound mixture into her oatmeal. Part of me didn't think it would work, an' the other half wished with all my soul that me Sophie would wake up transformed, for the better." Hazel intensely stirred the contents of her pot as if she were preparing potion for another ritual.

"So, did it work?" I was entertained, but Granny's narrative was moving slow—I assumed for dramatic effect.

"You tell me if it worked. My daughter may have endured the infirmities of the weak, but her heart never changed. An' somehow, she got a second chance. Or should I say, she made one." Her revelation was followed by a billow of steam that rose from the contents of her pot as she poured them into a coffee mug. She placed the cup of rising vapors in front of me.

"Let me guess—this happened on her seventeenth birthday. Is this the poison you gave my mother?" I was terrified of the witch's brew.

"Silly girl…it's herbal tea." Was she serious?! She just told me my mother was a heartless bitch, which I totally believed, and she used old school Louisiana voodoo to teach her a lesson. Did she really think I was going to drink something she concocted? I think not!

"So you're telling me that your daughter, my mother, knows what I've been going through this whole time? What a cunt." My uncertainty of the aged lady who stood before me soon turned to confirmation of betrayal. It sunk in deep beyond my ears and traveled to my core where a relatable connection between myself and my grandmother occurred: a sympathetic connection neither one of us ever experienced with Sophie.

"Not only does she know, she only had ya to give it to ya." My mind reminisced back to my very first episode when Sophie told me to go get help. She wasn't requesting aid for Olivia, she was telling me to get help for myself. She knew Olivia would wake up and that I'd soon be plagued with cancer. I rewound the memories to the forgotten moments just before that. I never questioned why Sophie was in my room that night; she was always there, the evil shadow just outside my cracked bedroom door, watching and waiting.

"Did you let her run around helpless and alone too?" Hazel started this curse, but then what.

"They say hurt people hurt people, which is true. But in time, remorse makes you feel like shit, no matter how much you feel your actions are justified. I cried to me ancestors, but they no answer, an' Sophie eventually left me." Hazel would have taken it back if she could.

"What about my brother?" I thought maybe she put a spell on him too. I mean why else would a grown ass man still be living at home with his mother?

"I can only assume that maybe the curse couldn't be transferred to a male. I wished your father could have saved you, but at least he knew you were alive. A daughter should know her father and a father his princess, if even for a fleeting time." Hazel cautiously sipped the hot tea.

"You were the nurse." My grandmother tried to right her wrong by contacting my father. Pretending to work at the hospital ran in the family.

"Milon was a successful man at one time, but seemingly that all disappeared once he met Sophie. No telling what she did to him." Clearly, playing a role didn't skip a generation. An actor disguised as a mother, my mother, was one hell of a character. I had officially hired Shonda Rhimes as the new head writer and executive producer of my life; this shit was scandalous. I needed a minute to process it all. I called Olivia to check in on Fate to see if she was minding her manners. I then headed to my childhood home to verify my mother's evil behavior. But would she admit her wrongs?

# illuminating the dark

Why are the evilest of human beings—although calling them human is contradictory—granted the right to reproduce without restriction? Just imagine if my grandmother could have proved to a therapist that her daughter was a nut job, preventing parental rights. Funny how people need a license to operate a vehicle, or even a permit from a licensed professional to add an addition to their house, but zero prerequisites to be an influential parent. It was a crap shoot—I could have gotten the good, the bad, or the ugly. I believe both men and women should have to undergo a psychological evaluation to ensure mental competency, and possible motives, to bring an unexpecting life into their fucked up world. That might be hypocritical, considering I recently unintentionally pushed a human through my vagina without a doctor's pre-approval note, but my compassion for a defenseless child superseded my selfishness. I didn't need a doctor to diagnose my unconditional love; it was innate. Parenthood brings out the best in people and, unfortunately, the worst.

I found myself entering my childhood home, determined to release Sophie of her theoretical paternal rights.

"Hello. Anyone home?" I called out into the soundless house and waited for a reaction; it was still. I sauntered the dim halls and ended up in my old room, which was unrecognizable. The bed I never made, the photos tacked to the walls, my clothes, and even the bottle of rum me and Olivia lifted from a store—everything I remembered was gone. Sophie controlled, alted, and deleted me. And just what was so significant that she had to remove my existence to make space for? I fed my hunger for nosiness by passively perusing papers on top of the desk. A few sheets in explained what to do after a mole removal procedure: *keep a layer of petrolatum (Vaseline) and a bandage on the wound.* My mummy in deed was a liar—chemical peel my ass. I wondered what else she was fabricating. I opened the filing cabinets of the built-in home office that occupied the room. There had to be over a hundred folders in the first drawer, and everything looked uninterestingly the same. But just as I began to move on and snoop in another drawer, something caught my eyes. An alphabetized tab that read *Anthony's Legal Docs* was attached to a folder full of lawful gibberish. In his thirty-four years, my brother had his fair share of arrests and lawyers, and behind those attorney's paid invoices was another type of statement for services provided. Blah, blah, blah… *Department of Child Services*. My hunger was more than fed; I was astonishingly pop belly full with the tea that overflowed from the pages.

"The application and all evidence for determination of suitability to adopt a child has been reviewed. It has been determined that you, Sophie Dubois (age 18), meet the eligibility requirements as the adoptive mother of Anthony Phillips." I wasn't sure what I expected to find, but that, that blew my mind. I didn't want to believe that Sophie tried to assume an already forgotten little soul just to add to his misfortune, but that's exactly what she fucking did. Further investigation was in order.

"This approval describes the following characteristics of said child in regards to age, gender, and health status: Male child with no known medical conditions at the age of three (3)." Okay, how was that even possible? How the hell could a teenager adopt a child? Well, my eyes racing over Sophie's research materials answered my question; You must be at least 21 years old to become a foster parent and at least 18 years old to adopt a child. You must be able to meet your needs and the needs of said child. You can be married, single, divorced, widowed, or be a co-parent. You can rent or own, but you must have adequate space available and your landlord's approval. You may ask for the age and gender of children you think would fit in best with your family situation and needs." I read deeply and intensely like I was reading this novel, but abruptly recognized that I wasn't alone. A spider dropped in alarmingly close and whispered terror in my ear. The feeling and absurd thought that it laid eggs, bit me, and planned to take over my body all at once sent me into a dramatic conniption. I jumped around like an elephant in an antique shop, things crashed down one after the other: picture frames, stapler, pens. I was so loud, I might as well have rang the church bell of shame to serenade Sophie during her walk of atonement.

"Get it together, Chance!" I calmed myself only after slapping my ear red. My need to establish more facts surpassed my fear of creepy crawly insects. I just hoped no one heard me. My experience as a skilled and inconspic-uous detective was limited to reruns of Law & Order. Too bad I didn't watch When Animals Attack; the com-bination of the two would have made me a smoother criminal. My lack of investigative techniques didn't deter me from prying and minding someone else's business. I couldn't resist further exploration of Sophie's orga-nized diary. Maybe she knew the eighth wonder of the world: why Oprah never married Stedman. I vigilantly slinked over to another cabinet where my fingers fer-vently skimmed; ultimately, I pushed all of the hanging folders to the left side and found a jewel tucked beneath. A tattered vintage trapper keeper held years of research: ripped pages of spells, rituals, and countless hand written records. The dated transcripts revealed similar rituals to the one Hazel told me she performed to set the whole damn mess in motion. With each of Sophie's attempts, she added or removed an element. She was persistent to remove the curse to say the least.

"Determined that failure to transfer to sacrifice was not due to gender but deficiency of blood relation. Sacrifice is obsolete…what a waste!" Sophie's penman-ship was aggressively heavy. It was dated just two days after Anthony's seventeenth birthday. I was born ten months later. Large numbers floated through my head like a familiar counting episode of Sesame Street. How could someone be so savagely calculating? She spent over a decade using Anthony as a guinea pig just to conclude him useless and inadequate. Possibly another folder would tell me why she kept him around years and years after he was of no more use to her. Copies of cashed checks made out to Sophie from a Dr. Dietrich Anschuetz are what I found next. Why did that name sound so familiar? Attached to the scanned copies were emails between the two.

"Although the questionnaire you submitted was inadequate, the medical records you also provided gave great insight into the compatibility and functionality of the patient's organs and healing abilities. Per our agreement, we will take possession of Chance Dubois for medical experiments, research, and extraction." Oh shit, Sophie sold me out to those fucking neo-nazis scientists in Germany. The second email confirmed that their attempts to take possession of me failed. Could they have been the men in those black vans? Sophie was evil: a deceiver leading all of us astray—also known as Satan. My attention was so deep in the depths of hell that I didn't notice the silhouette of a woman in the doorway. Her subservient beady eyes didn't stray from mine while her arm reached and flicked the light switch. It was Denise. She didn't speak or scream bloody mary. She just stood there and scanned the tower of documents I had stacked like Jenga, contemplating her next move. Denise peacefully walked away without removing a block. I guess she didn't want to play, and just maybe she was going to find someone who did. With the lights on, it made it easier to snoop. I put my flashlight phone down, freeing both my hands to furtively investigate. The deed to the house in which I stood was signed and transferred to Sophie Dubois the year I was born. The legal document proved that ownership was previously held by Milon Smith. Six additional pieces of real estate were signed over from my father to my mother that year. Either Sophie had the best pussy on the planet, or she slipped her baby daddy one hell of a drug. It had to be a substance a lot more potent than love potion number nine; a fucking bear tranquillizer seemed legit. It was the only way to get a man to sign over his assets and his parental rights.

"What are you looking for?" The monster's servant, and not-so-obsolete sacrifice, caught me with my hands in his mother's cookie jar. Before reading his adoption papers, a fraction of my mind made him guilty by association. But thereafter, there was no way he was privy to the conspiracy. Just as Sophie didn't divulge her master plan, I too really didn't have the patience to explain myself, or to fill my brother in on the cluster-fuck that was our family. Anthony couldn't possibly handle all of the evidence I had scattered around the workspace—at least not all at once. He only needed one logical revelation at that moment, but was it my secret to tell?

"Oh hey, Brother. I'm just untangling the sinister threads that our mother has selfishly woven. She was cursed, and when she couldn't pass that curse on to her son, she gave birth to a second chance. Oh and by the way, I have supernatural abilities to cure cancer, and you're adopted and she's probably kept you around as her devoted minion supporting you and wiping your ass because she took a liking to you and felt some kind of guilt in that fucked up cold heart of hers." I could have been reckless with the facts, but I sympathetically thought about my words before they hit the air and stabbed his heart. He may have been a grown ass man, but hurt is hurt no matter the age. And true family is family no matter the blood. He looked confused—as anyone would be—so I revised my approach.

"Do you know who Anthony Phillips is?" I could tell by the strange wrinkle of his face that his birth given name didn't ring a bell. I gathered up the pile of facts and handed him his truth before leaving the room. It was time to confront the evil puppet master.

# let's play russian revenge

A player of a premeditated game can be so intently focused on the objective of winning that they fail to inform their opponents that the game has begun, thus being a cheater. By forcing her punishment upon me, she thought she'd won. On the contrary, the pieces on my side of the chessboard never moved; a loser had yet to be determined. And although Sophie gave herself a wicked head start, I wasn't going to hold it against her. It's said that the only way to win with a toxic person is not to play—fuck that. I decided to join in the fuckery and present a competitive challenge. Strategically, I'd place her under an inescapable threat of capture and then watch her beg for mercy…

checkmate bitch! For it's not how one started, but how they ended. I think Mr. Miyagi said that inspirational shit in one of the Karate Kid movies, but I didn't pull inspiration for my next move from the karate master. I took leadership from the ultimate bitch of retribution. What would karma do?

I lightly snuck up to Sophie's bedroom door; it protruded slightly enough for me to witness she and her housekeeper carrying out their nightly routine. Denise passed Sophie facial wipes to remove the dirt, oil, and thick foundation from her face. It looked like a box of crayons threw up on the four or five cleansing towelettes. A chemical peel and makeup? I think not—the way she had her face wrapped like a Christmas gift, there's no way she could parade around a face full of makeup the next day. Sophie had taken her mask off, but the show had just begun. My self-confidence scrambled with apprehensive anxiety made for an appetizing state of emotions; my bubbled guts wanted to be the brown cherry on top. It was either run to the bathroom or face my demons—although they both seemed one in the same at that moment. I entered my mother's room with assertiveness at the forefront and clenched butt cheeks behind me.

"Would that be Pine-Sol or chemotherapy you're intravenously injecting into my mother's arm?" I questioned the so-called housekeeper who was moonlighting as Sophie's in-home nurse. I caught the caregiver and her client off guard. Denise kept her employers little secret and refrained from speech as she left the master bedroom.

"I wasn't expecting you, Chance." Sophie connivingly spoke out into the dimly lit room, hiding like a wolf in grandmother's nightclothes. I walked closer to her. What big freckles she had, proving what big lies she'd told.

"We all deserve a chance, don't we mom? Maybe two or three." I uninvitingly sat on the bed and began to read her a bedtime story.

"Once upon a time there was a girl who had a few M&M's, and she was so eager to share her M&M's with someone else, that she searched high and low for the right person—the only person who could accept the M&M's from her and know exactly what to do with them."

"I'm not sure I'm following your story. You know I don't like candy," Sophie interrupted me.

"And by candy, you mean cancer, right? And by M&M's, I mean a few malignant melanomas that are attacking your body. Melanoma occurs when the pigment-producing cells that give color to the skin become cancerous; how ironic. And you expect me to cure you of your cancer, right?" Pieces of my narration were compliments of Sophie's very own medical cliff notes that I'd found in her office. My audience's face told me that she was not entertained by my storytelling. I continued; hopefully she'd like the way the story ended.

"Instead of taking your punishment, you found a way out by taking advantage of two innocent children and then craftily got the prodigal child to return home to heal you yet again. But there's a plot twist:enter a remorseful fairy grandmother with hazel eyes, who enlightens this prodigal child about the purpose of her life."

"Okay, I get it—you've talked to Scar Face, and now you know why I had you and why I brought you back." Sophie realized the game was no longer to her advantage.

"Should the prodigal child heal her selfish ass mother?" Continuing in third person offered dramatic effect.

"She should if she loves her. I gave you a great life… you owe me." I straddled her just like she wanted me to.

"Just relax, we'll both feel better soon." But me pinning her hands to the sheets below her was unfamiliar.

The stage four cancer made her too weak to physically contest.

"Chance, that hurts." Elevated panic pushed blood to the surface of the whites of her eyes. The polluted reflection revealed her empty, unapologetic soul.

"Once you brought kids into the world, adoptive or otherwise, it wasn't about you anymore." I spoke up for me and my brother.

"My mother made me just as ugly as she was; this is all her fault. You would have done the same thing." Her forceful statement spewed saliva onto my face. Pleading for her life or any sign of loving empathy was nonexistent; neither one of us possessed the capacity for rationalism that night. Revenge was required.

"Granny and I have a something for you, we figured out how to re-gift all that you've given to me. Ever thought about what would happen if the curse was reversed to the diseased host who currently has one foot in a cancerous grave? The rapid increase of freckled fragments just might cause an explosion." The chanted vengeance might have sounded familiar to Sophie.

*"I reflect the harm that is placed on me*
*Let evil eyes see beauty*
*And wicked words replaced with sympathy*
*Attract the pain of the weak for all of eternity*

*A mark upon your face will be your loving reminder*
*That a cruel soul should be remorseful and kinder*
*Bind the dark heart and negativity of the mother I call Sophie*
*Protect me with light and love—so shall it be."*

"Give me a chance to explain…" Sophie aggressively hungered for air, and an accelerated impulse delivered a bolt of energy like a paddle connected to a defibrillator. Abruptly her struggle declined; her body fell limp. Both our faces splattered: our freckles freckled with blood. I didn't truly believe—my threats were just to scare her. I lied; Hazel and I made no plans of retaliation. I wanted truth and heartfelt confessions. But if talking shit was my only revenge, what the fuck just happened? I unlocked my disturbed red eyelids to examine the gruesome demise that I didn't anticipate. With the destructive penetration of a single bullet, red liquid emptied from my mother's head and covered the starched sheets like a fresh coat of paint. What do you do when your mother's love is deceitfully conditional and built on evil and shitty foundation? You send her back to hell. Gunpowder layered Anthony's hands, terror molded his face, and pained tears soaked his cheeks. No spiritual witchcraft, ritual candles, consecrated chants, ancestry roots, or devilry—just a son scorned. A great deal of deception was more than cruelly piercing and, once the truth was exposed, it all became fatal. Deadly. The gun fell to the floor, and so did my brother. The unrestricted sensation of love he once devoted to Sophie was now nonexistent. I'm not sure what all he comprehended from the documents I shared with him, but what he read in that short amount of time didn't sit right with his soul—his infliction of retaliation came swift. Ding-dong, the witch was dead.

"Anthony!" I shouted his name. I wasn't sure if I felt cheated that he stole my revenge or relieved that it didn't take place at my hands. It was easy for me to tend to my brother, leaving my mother's body and disregarding the relationship's demise, seeing as though it was one sided from the beginning. With the grief brushed underneath my heart's rug, I met Anthony on the floor where he thawed from shock. After I soothed his face with my hands and kiss upon his forehead, he looked me in my eyes matter of factly and insisted I leave the scene of the justified crime.

"Go. Go be with Fate. You were never here." Anthony pushed me away and towards the one I unreservedly loved and who legitimately loved me. No spells, no potions, no lies—just a pure love between mother and child: something the two of us had missed out on.

"I can't just leave you," I said the words but I truly wanted to get the hell out of that house.

"Go now." This time the order came from the second in demand. Denise pulled me up to my feet and pressed me to vacate the premises as well. This chick was quick to switch sides; or maybe she favored Anthony's side long before I arrived. I left, and used one of Fate's wipes from my purse to erase Sophie's blood from my face.

I'd just lost my mother and seemingly my brother, and all I could think about was squeezing my daughter. I went straight to Olivia's house to get her.

"Mommy!" She ran to me like I never ran to Sophie. Our love for each other was more than powerful: it was intentional. Her amplified heart rate thumped through her chest with happiness. And so did mine.

"Owie, Mommy." I thought that I held her so intensely tight that it hurt her, but when I released her tiny body she revealed her gauzed forearm. Olivia followed with explanation.

"I'm sorry, it was my fault. I left a burning candle in the room when I left to use the bathroom, came back and she had already been burned. The cool water reduced the swelling. I cleansed the affected area with soap and applied some ointment. She stopped crying the moment I wrapped it, so I didn't think she needed real medical treatment." She was more than apologetic like her own child had been burned. Given what I just experienced, the severity was minuscule in my eyes.

"Let me see, Princess. Does it hurt?" I gently catered to the minor injury by pulling the dressing back with ease.

"Oh shit." Fate's threshold for pain had reached its max only because the enormity of her physical strength was exposed; the burn was healed with only a trace of a single freckle.

The Dubois family fuckery continued.

*about the*
## author:

TAMIKA JORAI is an imaginative virtuoso, or obnoxiously insane—she's undecided. An advocate of anything that leads to thoughtful laughter, she dedicates her life to genius cinemas, candy, and unicorns that smell like bacon. Somehow, the combination of the three distorts her reality and makes for an amusing storyteller. *Freckled Face* is her debut fictional tale, and unquestionably not her last. Follow Tamika Jorai on social media @freckledface_fuckcancer or visit her website at www.tamikajorai.com